THE FIRST OF A FOUR BOOK SET

I0537924

Part I   *10000 Meals*

Part II   *20 Years of New Earth*

Part III   *The Diaries of Terri and Mia Johnson*

Part IV   *The Holiday of Pie Johnson*

ISBN: 978-1-941263-07-5

DON'T MISS THESE OTHER HOT NOVELS BY PA BUCKLEY

- The Witch
- The Dead Have No Need For Money
- Ah... to be Dead
- It Is The Right Hand... That Kills
- Skeletons
- Tempest
- Doctor Incubator

10000 MEALS

PA Buckley

Tickets to Paradise

As the rocket ship soared into the atmosphere, earth's time was almost over. The plan was for a million such missions, each rocket crammed with a thousand people. After breaking free from earth's gravity, the passengers would be transferred, taking up residence in larger space station style ships that would slowly accelerate away to the furthest reaches of the Universe. The destinations were small, earth like planets that could support life... well, it was hoped. For some the trip would take a lifetime, others would only be in space for as brief as three years. That shorter – and more pleasant time frame – was slated for the occupants of rocket ship XJ 222-4.

The mood among the passengers was upbeat to say the least, as the thrusters fired up, and with a tremble and shake, the ship began its rise. They were the lucky ones. Only a few hundred ships had been built and this was the first to contain the common man. That meant there were no billionaires, heads of state, or those connected to the well healed on board. XJ 222-4 held a collection of ordinary folk. It was true, college degrees were common among the passengers, but not earned from those exclusive schools known as the playgrounds of the rich. The passenger list was a wide mix of men, women, and children from a variety of social backgrounds.

The trip itself was little more than a junket, barely breaking the upper crust before rendezvousing with the massive space station that, powered by dual nuclear engines, would make the long term journey to a distant planet. These were not ordinary space stations, similar to the ones that orbited Earth. Instead they were designed to hold a payload equivalent of five rocket ships, or five thousand people, with large food bins stored with prepackaged meals to feed the occupants on the trip's first phase. The frozen meals would be supplemented with large gardens, designed to grow the additional groceries needed, for even as big as the ships were, such quantities of food were beyond their payload. The only way to justify more extended trips was to recover and recycle the food and water held onboard.

Although none of the passengers had been specifically informed, this rocket was stocked with the worker bees. It would be the future rockets that delivered the rich and well connected. These later arrivals would make the trip in ease, passing their three years of travel as if on a luxury cruise liner. Further it had already been determined, once arrived at their destination, they would be the ruling class, continuing the informal master-slave relationship that had secretly been brokered when the original flight plans were drawn up.

Even the rocket ships transporting them to the space station were different. Far more secure, there would be no "Sally Ride" moment for the upper caste, with the rocket exploding before reaching the space station. This was even reflected in the seating, where the occupants of the first rocket ship, XJ 222-4 – XJ4 for short – were deposited within like cattle and strapped in using seatbelts little better than a compact automobile. But for the other three rockets; XJ1, XJ2, and XJ3, each seat had the look and feel of a NASCAR racecar. There was to be no XJ5. That launch had been scuttled to provide more room for the ruling class and their valuables.

The last three rocket ships would be joining Space Station 222, or SS 222 as it was known, only after the ship had been prepared, making their arrival as stress free as possible. Already its sister space station, SS 221, carrying the wildlife and flaura and fauna to be transported, had departed, along with a much smaller ship that held a water transformer, a necessary machine that could convert the hydrogen and oxygen heavy air of the desert like planet into life sustaining water.

As for their destination, the planet they would be colonizing – labeled ELS 107 –was considered among the best with regards to potential. Four hundred and eighty six planets had been identified as potentially hospitable for human life, each one classified and rated on its ability to sustain life as known on Earth. ELS 107, the one hundred and seventh planet identified, had earned the preferred label of "ELS," which signified "Earth Like Sustainability." And of all planets earning an ELS rating, ELS 107 was the second highest rated.

The grading system was simple. Each was given numerical score based upon similarities to earth, including such measurements as length of year, length of day, distance from the related sun like star, planet diameter, oxygen content in the atmosphere, and water on the planets crust. There were a myriad of other metrics included in the calculation, but those were some of the most basic.

Planet ELS 107, the new earth they would be sailing to, had a rating of 1.12. The closer to 1.00, the better. There were only five planets with scores marking close to 1.00, with only ELS 254 at 1.03 scoring better than ELS 107. Therefore, New Earth was an option for only the richest and closest connected to the inner circles of power. As such, the animal and plant cargo of SS 221 was of the highest quality. The three rocket ships that were to follow would include a treasure trove of private valuables, including gold, silver, and platinum. Things the wealthy passengers thought might be of value anywhere in the Universe. Due to the added weight, these rockets would launch with half the total passengers – five hundred each. Added to that were cats, dogs, hamsters, designer clothing, and anything else the wealthy deemed to be valuable.

This of course meant that upon departure, SS 222 would only be carrying two thousand five hundred instead of the full capacity of five thousand. There were no complaints from the upper class over the reduced passenger list, who preferred comfort and their money over saving lives. If that upset the proletariat, then so be it. After all, their destination was literally light years away. They were traveling to paradise and were focused on future glory, not those stuck in the current disaster they were escaping.

The docket schedule indicated tomorrow as the date the rockets loaded with the rich would depart earth. For now, they were lining their rockets with goods and valuables when word passed among them. XJ4 had successfully launched and would soon be docking with SS 222. A cheer went up, but it wasn't very loud or enthusiastic . The well bred and wealthy don't behave in such ways. No need to. When fortune smiles upon them, it is expected, not applauded. And after all, they had valuables to store and trinkets to hide. That was certainly more important that jumping about and acting the part of a fool.

It was little over an hour before XJ 4 docked with SS 222; the hermetic seal broken and the doorway opened. As the passengers filed in, directions were barked out as two conductors guided them to the dining area. Not that a meal was about to be served, rather this was the largest room on the spaceship, the most suitable for convening a meeting and crowd control. It was easy to observe the smiles of happiness and feelings of joy. They had made it. This was where everyone wanted to be, on a ship heading away from earth. And it didn't hurt to be in a gravity free environment. As the passengers floated along toward the dining areas, the ship had an amusement park like atmosphere. The space station's artificial gravity wouldn't be activated until the other three rockets had arrived to allow for proper docking procedures.

When released from the dining area, the passengers were to stow their belongings below their assigned bunks, no more than fifteen pounds per person, placed on their laps for the ride up. There would be no private rooms or cordoned off areas for the new arrivals. Those accommodations were reserved for tomorrow's rocket ships. But no complaints were made or heard. Only voices of excitement and joy. One doesn't complain after winning the lottery. Once settled in and attendance taken, they would be dispatched to their assigned jobs. Just a brief stopover to familiarize themselves with the ship, nothing more. And afterwards… a well-earned meal.

Before any of that could take place, a safety walkthrough the ship had to be completed. Inspecting for stress fractures would take precedence over stowing belongings, job assignments, or eating. This inspection was a job that fell to the Johnson family. Gordon was a structural engineer and his wife Terri worked for the powerful Senator Larry Fillmore. When she saw that someone was going to have to check the integrity of the SS 222, she immediately saw the chance to save her family. They would all earn tickets onto SS 222, complements of her husband's degree. Once he was approved and certified, she forged the other three spots for herself and their two children. After all, it was a simple job and Gordon assured her he was up to the task for all four. In fact, most ships had only one structural engineer, but the SS 222, had orders for an additional three. At least that was how the requisition form read once Terri finished the paperwork.

No doubt, the Senator would arrive on a later rocket ship and she would be found out. But her logic was simple. Better to be alive onboard SS 222 and yelled at than suffer as others, where a one family member made it on board, knowing the rest of the family were doomed. She didn't want to make such a decision, and couldn't if she were forced to. So as they disembarked onto SS 222, when the conductor shouted, "Blue Team!" she grabbed her son Jon while Gordon took daughter Mia's wrist and they floated to the side as directed. The conductor gave them a surprised look, but Terri, anticipating such a reaction, thrust the papers toward him. After a brief perusal, the conductor said, "Alright. If that's what it is, then get going. We can't do anything until you finish your going-over."

Gordon nodded. "Don't worry. Won't be long. Just a simple routine walk around. Nothing that should take too long."

Jon, trying to be clever, said, "Or float around."

Gordon glanced sternly at Jon, saying grimly, "Yes… or float around."

Watching as the four family members disappeared down the long hallway, the conductor grumbled, "Good, I'm getting hungry," before returning to his assigned checklist. There was still work to do before he would get his meal, or anyone else for that matter.

The Walk Around

It was really quite simple. Using a light touch and a sharp eye as they passed through the space station, Gordon occasionally stopped to examine the struts, welds marks, and braces that were the spaceship's main supports. If anything was wrong, Gordon was to log it in. The paperwork was much more detailed than that, but in reality even if major structural concerns were discovered, nothing more could be done.

The written guidelines were specific. If any structural problems were discovered, SS 222 would be taken off line and a maintenance crew assigned to complete the necessary repairs. But with the situation deteriorating on Earth, there would be no time for such safety measures. Unless a severe structural problem was discovered that clearly classified the ship as unsafe – and by unsafe that meant guaranteed to explode or rip apart – SS 222 would be leaving orbit from planet Earth tomorrow.

So why conduct the walk around? That was how they had made it onto the ship, labeled as structural engineers, and Gordon didn't want to do anything that might jeopardize their rights on the spaceship. On Earth, things were still fairly under control, but it would be foolish to describe the situation as stable. Now that they were on the space station, it would be hard to process a removal order considering the short time frame before launch. But why jeopardize their position? Much better to follow the rules, silly as they were, and ensure staying on board. In case anyone was secretly observing, either on camera or otherwise, Terri had trained the children for this exercise. Serious faces and a business like attitude were needed. So as they moved through the cavernous ship, both children – clipboard in hand – darted their eyes about with grim faces as if certified and experienced inspectors.

The first section of the ship to be reviewed were the gardens, large rooms with long steel troughs bolted to the floor. Entering the room, Gordon was surprised to see that not only had the gardens not been seeded and watered, but no dirt had been placed in the troughs that were to serve as the beds for the fruits and vegetables. Due to the ship's current weightless status, the troughs were supposed to be covered with long plastic sheets. Instead all that was visible were empty molded steel trenches with thin metal tubes with nozzles above that were to distribute the water. Gordon made a detailed note so that when the dirt was found crews could be commissioned to transfer the dirt straight away to the gardens. After all, once the prepackaged meals were exhausted, this would be everyone's sole source of food.

But lack of food shouldn't be a problem. The rich customers who purchased passage on board SS 222 had included payment for additional provisions that should cover for the entire three years. That, and the reduced passengers list made the gardens little more than an added amenity. Still, this had to be noted. The space station needed to be balanced properly for the trip. If the dirt wasn't there, calculations would be needed and something... bodies, food, or other items of mass, shuffled about. The space station had to be in proper equilibrium. An unbalanced ship would sail off course. Considering they would be traveling many light years to their destination, even a hundred thousandth of a degree would result in missing the final destination by millions of miles.

After a quick check showed all four garden rooms empty, Gordon said, "Ok, let's go. Nothing more to see here."

Next were the passenger quarters, split into coach, second class, first class, and premium. The coach rooms were little more than large square boxes with a hundred bunk beds lined tightly against the walls. Inside each was a small box for personal belongings and no lock. Too much weight. The second class rooms were little better with the same style of bunk beds but fewer to the room. Both coach and second class were limited to communal bathrooms and showers.

First class was better, with four beds total – a three story high bunk bed and a separate twin size bed – all in a single room. There was more space to move about, but only barely and they too would be assigned to the commune type bathrooms. But while coach and second class had one cramped bathroom for a thousand people, first class – which consisted of one thousand seven hundred and forty eight beds – had five bathrooms to share among them. These bathrooms came with better amenities such as walls between the showers and toilets.

The second highest in quality were the premium rooms. Two hundred forty beds, each with its own individual room, only slightly bigger than the bed, and each cluster of four beds had a common room almost six feet by six feet with a door that could be locked. For every sixty beds there was a single bathroom.

That left the ten super premium bedrooms, similar in style to a hotel room with a king size bed, sofa that rolled out to another bed, bureau for clothing, and small but private bathroom.

As Gordon led his family through the living quarters, no structural concerns were observed, but again something was missing. No mattresses on the beds. The shipping orders stated each bed was to have a mattress, folded and tied to the bed, along with one set of sheets and a pillow. Instead they found cold steel. That was also the case for coach, second class, first class, and premium. Further, none of the sofas or bureaus had been installed. Just empty rooms with lightweight steel bed frames.

"Gordon, where are the mattresses? What are the kids to sleep on?"

"Must be stowed away somewhere. I'll note that."

"Yes, we need that by tonight. I don't want them sleeping on hard metal."

"Neither do I."

"Yes, well I'm speaking to the Captain. This just won't do."

"Hush!"

"But…"

"Be quiet. You'll talk to no one."

"How you talk! I'm not a maid."

"Yes… keep quiet. Right now at least. They can bring a shuttle over here right quick and then where will we be?"

"Oh that is ridiculous. We're already on."

"And I want to keep it that way. You want to return to Earth?"

"No... you know that."

"Then for now keep your opinions to yourself. Once we arrive on New Earth and are established, you can speak all day. But for now... hold your tongue."

"Really! I think now..."

"I know! You think quite enough of yourself. I've had enough experience of that for ten lifetimes."

"I was the one who got us on here."

"Thank you very much. But you're not going to be the one to get us thrown off... things are shaky right now, there are literally millions of people who would take our positions, billions in fact. Those people are going to die. We aren't going to do anything to jeopardize that. What I heard just before we left is that everything's falling apart. I could have sworn I heard gunfire when we were boarding. More ships are coming tomorrow, it would be easy to put us on them, and send us back. You want that?"

"No."

"Then we stick to the script. If there are no pillows, we find a way. Period."

Terri glared angrily at Gordon, but he was right. Staying on Earth was a death sentence. There was no way around that. Gordon was usually right about these things. She could always lodge a complaint in a few days. But she didn't want to just give in.

"Where's the mattresses? They must be somewhere?"

"Yes. We are going to check the rest of the ship. We'll find them."

"Sure?"

"Yup. Says here to check everything. We'll come across them."

"And if we don't?"

Gordon smiled at Terri, rapping on the metal wall. "Then get used to sleeping on this. Where are the computers for that matter? Each premium room is supposed to have one, big screen as well."

She frowned before moving away without comment.

Next were the kitchens, sparse and plain. Nothing more than microwaves to heat the food and plastic utensils… forks, knives and spoons and plates, all of it cheap and lightweight. There was a galley for ovens and stoves, but those too were missing. After a few taps on the hull, Gordon said, "Let's go. Only the engine room, food stores, and the bridge and steering room left."

Stopping at the engine room door, with the red, yellow, and black warning sign indicating nuclear radiation inside, Gordon said, "Hold here. I'll be the only one to go inside."

"Why's that Pop," asked Jon.

"Because son, I got my kids."

"What's that mean?"

"It means stay here."

Entering, there was a large nuclear reactor to each side amid the slight glow of the engine room. They had been advertised as being able to work for a thousand years, but Gordon knew better. A little research on his part had discovered a life more around two hundred years. It was supposed to have been turned on several days ago to warm the energy rods and glancing in a small circular window a few inches wide with a thick plate of leaded glass inserted, Gordon could see a dim red light as if an ember of coal in a barbeque pit. He quickly moved on and after a few taps checked the integrity of the walls, returning outside. He knew enough about uranium to know it was dangerous stuff.

"Daddy, why are you sweating?"

"No reason Mia. Stay with your mother. Come on, let's check the food stores."

"Food! Cool," said Jon, "I'm hungry."

"Me too," said Terri, "But we got to do our job first."

"Come on kids," said Gordon, "I'm hungry too. The faster we do this, the sooner dinner comes."

"Dinner sounds good daddy," said Mia, "I'll race you."

Gordon laughed. There was no one around and it was good to have the kids so happy. After all the stress they had gone through it was nice to see his family happy. Tough times were ahead, that was sure. But that prospect was better than the last several months, when he woke up every day to the thought that death would soon take his family, the result of a choking heat baking everyone to death.

How does one answer the question, "Are we going to get cooked alive?" Gordon smiled grimly, you don't. Instead you had to get a ticket on a rocket ship escaping Earth.

Mother Earth

The first signs of trouble came in the form of earthquakes and tsunamis. Of course global warning was considered the cause. But the conversation changed when the Mariana Trench, the deepest point in on the planet began to buckle. A thorough analysis made it clear that more was at work than missing some fluorocarbon particles in the sky. As the fault line continued to deepen, reaching the earth's magma core, a ridge of violent volcanoes began to erupt along a range over five thousand miles. At first it was advertised as Mother Earth playing her games, and exciting talks emerged of a new continent being formed. Of course Atlantis was the most popular name for the newly formed land. But as the source of the volcanic activity was identified, it appeared that the problems were much larger and deeper than suspected... for the first time, a hint of concern seeped into news reports.

A secret NASA research project returned a clear and simple conclusion. The Earth's mantle plates were shifting out of control and the string of volcanoes would continue to grow, heating the planet's surface to a temperature over five hundred degrees, eliminating all life. To be sure, stories popped up of those planning on burrowing into the earth's crust, creating settlements that would sustain them. But how many people could exist burrowed in the ground like bugs and worms? And for how long? Especially with the Earth heating up so quickly – up to a degree a week. Such high temperatures would ultimately turn the oceans, rivers, and lakes to vapor.

When the secret report leaked, as they always do, panic began to spread across the planet. To ease the people's concerns, leaders of the major countries announced organized plans for evacuation of large segments of the population. This was quickly followed by the marketing phrase, "A million ships – A thousand each." That wasn't quite accurate. The rocket ships were to be used up to a hundred times each with a total of ten thousand built. They would make roundtrip passages to space stations that would travel the long distance to the one of the four hundred eighty six planets identified as potential safe havens.

That was the plan presented to the public. Those who created and presented the proposal knew it was unrealistic, but it gave the impression that up to one billion people would be saved from death. In reality, there wasn't enough time to follow through with such a vast plan. But it achieved its real goal – placate the people – calming them with hope. Hope they might be one of the lucky ones who would make the lottery onto a space station departing for better worlds. It worked. Life returned to a more normal pace, relatively speaking. Rocket ships were built, space stations created, and people focused on trying to find ways to earn a place on the all-important list of those lucky enough to earn passage off earth.

The governments of the world even went so far as to imply that everyone who wanted passage off planet Earth would be accommodated. After the initial leak, security was tightened, and as more data indicated that the crack in the earth's outer shell was worse than expected, this fact was kept from the public. After all, what more could they do? Even working at full capacity, ten thousand reusable rockets couldn't be built to transport people off the planet, nor enough space stations for so many people even if the rockets delivered there targeted payloads.

While two hundred and fifty space stations had been built, most earlier versions were small, designed as advance rockets to prepare the target planets for colonization, some ships so small they held a crew of one. They were designed to use the latest technology, preparing the planets for human occupation… if possible. These small ships were destined for planets that might not be habitable. Many of the potential Earths – more like most of them, and possibly all – may actually be completely inhospitable for human life. Those who left on the advance team rockets understood the options. They would either perish in space, transform the landscape of their future planets, or die once arrived.

In all SS 222 was only the one hundredth full size carrier class space station built, designed to hold up to five thousand passengers. And of those one hundred built, many were filled not with humans, but plants and animals. More information withheld from the general public. After all, no one left to die would wanted to know they had been passed over for squirrels, birds, worms, ferns, and in some cases elephants, rhinos, and other exotic animals.

But the decision had been made, this had to be done. Without such species and plant matter, it was questionable that man would be able to survive on these new hostile worlds. Further, human beings were the informal caretakers of Earth. They had a duty to preserve earth, or some semblance of it. Data chips were nice for preserving facts and words. But that couldn't compare to real animals roaming free. What is the point of existing if it is only as an electronic file in a computer? There is something about the land we walk and air we breathe. Experiencing life in the brief period of time we are allotted to exist in the Milky Way. All big cities have zoos, but does that mean everything has to be locked up, hidden away, or read from a book? If fewer humans made the trip, the decision was, so be it. The majority of animals selected were based on their hardiness, variety, and ability to adopt to new environments. This thought process went all the way down to amoeba and bacteria, both good and bad. Humans were tough beings, but complex as well, requiring a vast variety of stimuli upon their being to exist.

As the project slowly progressed, the crack in the earth's outer shell continued to crumble. Time – which was already short – turned out to be less than anticipated. In fact, as XJ4 quaked its way into the air, surface temperatures were beginning to spike with readings of two hundred degrees and more at the equator, showing no signs of lessening. Tomorrow's rockets; XJ1, XJ2, and XJ3 would be the last to depart. As for the remainder of humanity, they were to stay behind on Earth, given no option but to wait, as the increasingly brutal atmosphere wrapped itself like a fireball around the planet Earth, cooking the life out of them like over baked biscuits.

The Food Storage Bins

The space station was designed with the food storage bins ringing the columnar shaped craft roughly halfway between the front and back of the ship. This decision was based on the simple mathematics of weight displacement. There were enough premade meals on board for the entire three year trip, and therefore food provisions easily made up the majority of the ships cargo. This in turn meant that for the ship to maneuver properly and remain in balance, the food stores had to be situated as centrally as possible. As the Johnson family continued along on their safety check, Mia chose to see how long she could float down the middle of the hallway, using her hands and feet as fins, swimming on a cushion of air. Jon took the opposite approach, planting his feet on whatever support he could find before launching himself as hard as possible into the open space, not concerned with direction, choosing instead to enjoy the experience of weightless flight.

Gordon and Terri drifted slowly behind, holding hands. Terri was enjoying the surreal moment while looking about at the surroundings, unaware that Gordon's mood was becoming blacker and blacker. Finally she glanced at him, observing a sneer. "Hey Mr. Sourpuss, why so glum?"

Gordon flashed his eyes at her, but said nothing.

"Come on, what is it? We got on. I won't say anything until were in space about pillows. Make you feel better?"

"No."

"Then what? Is New Earth hospitable? We got the best option possible. That's what I was told. Senator Fillmore wouldn't lie. I heard him on the phone. This is as close to earth as humanly possible. What more could you want?"

"Pillows."

"Pillows? Oh you're being silly. I was being silly. We'll sleep on cold steel if we have to."

"No, that's not what I mean. Pillows. Computers. Ovens. Were missing a lot. Who knows what else."

Terri looked away. Gordon could suck the fun out of anything, even surviving a horrible death of being baked to death. But then she took a moment to consider his words. He could be a real killjoy, but often was also right. She would never admit it, but listening to Gordon had steered them in the right direction much more often than not. Just as women have a sixth sense, so too Gordon had one… for impending trouble.

Heading away from the front of the ship they were approaching an intersection. "This is it," said Gordon, "The food aisle." The aisle they had been moving down ran the length of the space station and the crossroad was an aisle that rimmed the circular edge of the ship with numbered food bins on each side. Reaching the junction they could see on one side bins starting with the number "001" and went up, disappearing out of sight with the curve of the ship. On the other side they could see bins returning down, the last two numbered "199" and "200" and facing each other.

"How much are these supposed to hold?" asked Jon.

Staring off down the aisle Gordon said, "Depends on the meals, but… about fifty thousand each." Looking down the isle reminded him of row houses. Orderly, neat, each the same as the last, holding a symmetry that was both pleasant on the eyes and cold in its sameness.

"Fifty… thousand?"

"Yup. So they say."

"Why that must go back for hundreds of feet."

Laughing lightly Gordon said, "No. Not likely."

"But fifty thousand?"

"Pack 'em in tight. We're on a ship now. Things are done different so you better get used to it."

Jon nodded as if he understood. "And how long we on here?"

"Bout three years, give or take a few months. Could be longer. Never know."

"Wow! That's a lot of food."

"Yup. I hope so."

Stepping to the food bin with the number "001" spray painted in it, Gordon stared first at the keypad on the door, then at the notes on his clipboard. Eyeing the clipboard, he punched "SS001" into the number pad. Three loud beeps were heard and the light turned changed from red to green. Grabbing the latch Gordon frowned slightly and pulled on the door. A gust of cold air hit him, and as the door opened he could see food packed to the top.

"Yea!" said Terri, clapping loudly.

"Yeah," said Mia, "I'm hungry. Let's grab something and go."

"No," said Gordon, "We got work to do."

"Yes Mia," added Terri, trying to hide her excitement at seeing the food, "The sooner we finish, the quicker we eat. What's next Gordon? The bridge?"

"Um... no. We got more work here."

"Oh, yeah. We have to do our walk around."

"Float around!" corrected Jon.

"Yeah," said Gordon somberly, "That and a little more. Let's check some more of these food bins."

"Why?" asked Terri, looking at the double sided aisle of red lights, "It's all here."

Gordon frowned at Terri. She was bright, but the kind that never wanted to follow rules. That could be cute and clever at times, but got them in trouble too.

"Does it say to check all the bins?"

Gordon checked his clipboard. "No."

"Does it say to check the first one only?"

"Yup."

"Well then stop being so stuffy and do your check and let's go. I'm hungry. And so are you. And when you get hungry, you get grumpy."

Smiling, Gordon said, "Aright, you go that way, kids you go the other way, meet on the other side."

"Ok!" said Jon, "Mom. We'll beat ya."

Terri hesitated, glancing over at Gordon, but seeing Jon and Mia already taking off shouted, "Hey! No fair. That's cheating!" before taking off.

Seeing them darting away, pushing from one side of the wall to the other, back and forth, Gordon glided to the food bin "200." Typing in "SS200" into the keypad, it beeped three times and the red light turned green. Pulling open the door there was no rush of cold air. When the door opened to reveal its contents, it showed… nothing. Empty except for the dim lighting of a single bulb.

Gordon inhaled at the sight, held it slightly, then exhaling slowly. After all, most ships didn't have enough food for all of the occupants for the entire trip. In fact some only had enough for the beginning period of the flight to their new home. The refrigerators were to store food grown in the garden areas, as well as the meat from the pigs, chickens, and whatever else brought on board related to eating. But Terri had been very clear on this point. Senator Larry Fillmore, the legendary and powerful chairman of the Appropriations Committee, had wanted to have enough food for the entire trip, and then some if possible.

Moving in front of food bin "199" he punched in "SS199," waited for the three beeps, and opened the door. It was the same. Empty. He pushed inside, bumping into the wall, it was room temperature. Shoving against the wall to return outside, he grabbed the door handle to stop his inertia and closed the door. In the distance he could hear Terri laughing while the kids argued.

"No," said Jon, "We won. We got here first!"

"No," said Mia, "Mommy one. See? She got to the middle first."

"How's that?"

"See the number on the wall? One hundred ten."

"So?"

"Mommy said that's over halfway."

"How you figure that?"

"Come on Jon," said Terri, "What's half of two hundred?"

"Um, a hundred."

"And one ten is over one hundred. Yes?"

"Yeah."

"So you know."

Not wanting to accept defeat, Jon said, "I'm going to find Dad."

Punching in the code "SS002" three beeps rang out and Gordon opened the door to the second food bin. There before him was a handwritten sign on a piece of paper floating in the otherwise empty food bin. It said simply:

"Fuck You Asshole"

Spaceship

The space station, described in basic dimensions, is nothing more than a huge hollow cylinder, a huge soda can floating in space. The simple design was selected in part because of the limited building time available, but also because such large dimensions – four hundred feet long and eighty feet in diameter – allow only the most basic of shapes to be recreated.

The obvious reason for the ship's size was the large number of people contained within. But there was a simpler reason; gravity, or lack of it. Unlike the complex and multi-level starships on display in movies that look like floating high class hotels, SS 222 was essentially hollow, the living quarters built on the outside shell of the ship. The middle was empty except for air, four water tanks, and the honeycomb of braces holding the ship together. With machines on board to generate fresh oxygen – supplemented by plants once they were grown, there was no need for so much open space, except for gravity.

In most movies, ships create their own gravity, conveniently holding everyone in place. But SS 222 had no such convenience. And so the space station generated its own gravity, limited that it was, by generating spin as it moved along. Not much, enough to keep people situated on the floor and plants and dirt in the steel trenches.

SS 222 had a capacity of two hundred food bins on board, each five feet wide by ten feet tall and fifteen feet deep, large enough to hold roughly fifty thousand frozen meals in containers an inch high by six inches long by four inches wide. This allowed for enough storage for ten million meals, more than three a day for the three year journey for twenty five hundred people.

The hull was a combination of carbon, titanium, aluminum, and vanadium, not unlike a typical spaceship, while the inside structure was aluminum reinforced with hybrid steels and fused plastic. The nuclear engines rated to last five hundred years before a major overhaul would be needed.

Although not built for speed, these ships would be the fastest ever, that is if the technology worked. With the theories of the existence of wormholes definitively proven wrong, new ideas on how to travel in space had been tested out, and it was determined that the quickest form of travel was in another dimension. We live in four dimensions, length, width, height, and time. Existing in these dimensions are fairly basic. The shortest distance between two points is a straight line for instance. But science has found that this is not always true. We actually live in a warped space where the shortest distance between two points may be a curved line and even that basic math, such as one plus one, doesn't necessarily always equal two. That is because gravity pulls, twists, and bends the space around it.

The goal of the new space travel was to find a way to use gravity to not only bend space, but bend it back upon itself, revealing a doorway to another dimension. In this case the seventh dimension was where it was theorized that two points measured as a great distance apart as we know it could be almost beside each other. Therefore the flight plan for SS 222 was to move a great distance away from the Sun, turn around, and return headed directly at the Sun. With the engines on full, SS 222 would charge forward, using Jupiter to slingshot around and generate even more speed, and as it approached certain death of slamming into the Sun, the ship would take a path scraping just beside the Sun, reaching a speed where its mass would use gravity to create a bend in the four dimensions and let the ship slip temporarily into the seventh dimension.

Then, in this short amount of time before it slipped back to the four dimensions, the ship would make the passage to new earth. That was the theory at least. It sounded crazy, but as scientists on earth watched previous spaceships take this path, it seemed to work, or the ships were simply burned up by the Sun undetected by their instruments. They weren't sure, but with no other options the press releases stated emphatically a one hundred percent success rate was experienced.

But burning up as the ship approached the sun wasn't what concerned Gordon as his family floated back to him. Rather he was interested in the number of meals on board before the jump to the next dimension. Three years was a long time. They needed food, lots of it. Either that or dirt and seeds to grow their own. And that didn't consider water. Reviewing the checklist once more, he noticed there was nothing regarding a review of the water tanks. He scrawled "Review of Water Bins" on the paper. This had to be done. After all, no water… they couldn't go anywhere.

He entered a room beside the food aisle with a small window on the hull. Looking out, he got a partial view of the earth, not a very good one, but enough. It almost looked as if there was a red hue ringing the planet. The kind of red he guessed that came from extreme heat. No food or water? That was a disaster. There were three ships arriving tomorrow… fifteen hundred people. Who was going to load up a ship with water or food? Or return to Earth for help? Already it was reported there were few rocket ships left, and one recently burned up on reentry, due to the Earth's extreme heat.

More to the point, what good would be a return to Earth? It was common knowledge the time frame for escaping earth was shrinking. Who would possibly want to help load water on a spaceship – or food for that matter – for someone else when they were days from burning to death? No, any ships leaving now would most likely carry people. Maybe they could add some water or food, but not on the scale needed on SS 222. Fifty thousand meals, maybe more… That didn't sound too bad. But no water? He hated to think of it. Water was the number one necessity for a human being. Anyone who knew anything about our physiology understood that. No water… you die, plain and simple. As he returned to the food aisle, Terri, Jon, and Mia were waiting, everyone showing grins. Despite the potential forboding situation, Gordon smiled himself. Terri had pulled her hair out in all directions and Mia was sideways, as if lying on a bed of air, a hand holding her head up. But it was Jon who made Gordon laugh. He was upside down and had his arms crossed as if nothing was wrong. If only the same could be said of the food and water supplies.

Firefight!!!

Gunfire crackled outside the rocket as Senator Fillmore sat inside XJ1, the flagship for SS 222. He was staring down a large fleshy man – only introduced as Jamison – who had been very clear and blunt in his demands. The rockets couldn't take off without his ground crew. And since the current plan was to leave the ground crew behind to die once the rockets launched, no rockets would be leaving any time soon... not without the ground crews on board that is.

This declaration had been announced at four o'clock in the afternoon, and it was ten now. Since the negotiations had started, the weather had quickly deteriorated. Earlier in the day, forecasts had predicted a cooling off once the Sun went down. When this proved false, at eight o'clock, Dan Cooper, America's number one newsman, who had made himself the symbol of hope to overcome this tragedy had angrily stomped off the set after announcing he was, "Going home to feed my dog and put a bullet in my head." It didn't matter that he didn't have a dog, and in fact was racing off to his personally made bunker in the side of a mountain with an extensive cooling system, ambient lighting, water, with large gardens installed. Nor did it matter his departure occurred only after a final request for passage on a rocket was denied. What did matter was his announcement to give up had echoed over the nation's airwaves, setting off a rein of chaos. Shortly after his abrupt signoff, signs of civil disturbance broke out across the country, sparking the gun battles that were now raging on the rocket pad.

The gunfire could be broken into two groups. Those outside trying to break in for a place on one of the rocket ships. And those with tickets on the ships, aided by the ground crews hoping to hitch a ride and supplemented by the remaining soldiers of the brigade assigned to protect the tarmac and rocket ships... men and women foolish enough to provide supporting fire despite no apparent hope of getting a seat on a rocket ship.

Considering the circumstances of the situation, this was the hardest negotiation Senator Fillmore had ever experienced. If the rockets didn't take off and soon, the growing mass of attackers would overrun the tarmac and all would be lost. And based upon the constant chatter of gunfire picking up in volume, time was almost out.

Five hundred fifty. That was Jamison's number. He wanted his five hundred fifty people on the ship. A skeleton crew would be left behind to man the launches – those who had pulled the short straw so to speak – and to die. Senator Fillmore knew very well the longer he waited meant a higher danger of being overrun, but also reduced the number of passengers on board as well as ground crew members alive to occupy seats.

If it was a protracted negotiation, Senator Fillmore would have been confident of success over the puffy and nervous Jamison. This was, after all, what he did. Negotiate. Why if more time was available, by the time they were done, he'd have Jamison so beaten that he'd be demanding to stay behind and that none of his crew be allowed on board. That was how good Senator Fillmore was. But then among the constant, "Pop! Pop! Pop!" of gunfire, a loud "BOOM!" echoed through the cabin of the rocket. It was time and Senator Fillmore knew it. That loud, low explosion was most likely an artillery shell, or worse yet, a tank. The end game had arrived.

Immediately he ceded to Jamison's demands as follows. All of the approved ground crew – still living that is – would be given passage onto the rocket ship. If that meant overloading the rocket, so be it. On the point of overloading the rockets, he had held out because of concerns the heavily weighted rocket might not make it to the space station, but also that they might crowd the space station unduly. After all, Senator Fillmore had a plan. And it was a grand one at that. He saw himself as Emperor of New Earth. He would live as... no, not a god. But, surely something better than a Senator... more than the President. Possibly something more along the lines of Caesar.

To do that, he needed his people in control. The last thing he wanted was five hundred fifty non-believers – almost all male and extremely intelligent – challenging his authority. But it would take but one shot from a tank to take out a rocket ship. And that meant negotiating was over. As he acquiesced to of Jamison's demands the word went out. Abandon all positions beyond the immediate rocket pad and get inside. The doors were closing and the engines prepared to fire. Armed tanks aggressively moving forward have the effect of drastically moving up time frames. Almost immediately much of the gunfire ceased and soon people – men, women, and children – could be seen sprinting toward the rockets. The constant "Pop-pop-pop" of gunfire was soon replaced by a more compact and controlled spurts, often with potential rocket occupants dropping to the tarmac. As the first passengers and ground crew poured inside the rockets, the fringes of the tarmac were dotted with a small but growing army.

As people filed in, seats were taken not based upon assignment, but rather convenience. The rocket was standing in an upright position with the seatbacks parallel to the ground. So when the seats by the door were taken, people began climbing over the other chairs as if on a ladder. One gunshot rang out, then another, sending a man falling back to the ground. A warning voice shouted, "No guns! Put a hole in the ship – we'll all die!"

This was followed by another voice announcing, "There's enough seats. Just get yer asses in!" Warning sirens began to blare over the tarmac as the remaining mission control staff began to bypass normal protocol, ignoring the pre-launch safety checklist.

As the first booster rockets began to fire up, sending bright white sparks in the air, another sound could be heard. It was a combination of the rumbling of a large diesel engine mixed with what appeared to be the rattling of chains. Then bumping its way over a berm and coming into view was a tank, manned by angry members of the army brigade who were to be left behind. In a final verdict, they decided that if they were to stay, then no one should escape this hell. Almost as soon as it came into sight, with a loud "BOOM!" the cannon was fired. The shot was hasty and missed. As the engine gurgled loudly, the tank accelerated, knocking several small planes out of its way before crunching over a group of people charging the rockets.

As passengers screamed and clamored inside, Senator Fillmore said, "That tank will kill us all. Shut the doors. Shut them all!" The order was denied with a flood of people jamming the doorway as they pushed their way through. Still, despite the chaos, the screaming, and the difficulty of climbing up the hull of a spaceship, it wasn't long before one rocket, followed by the others, clanked their hatches closed and confirmation was shouted to the tower, "Ready for liftoff!"

"Boom!" Again the tank fired its cannon. After a few short seconds of a whistling the shell slammed into one of the rockets fuel tanks. But it didn't explode as expected, instead sending fuel gushing out, draining down the side of the rocket. Realizing if the rocket exploded on the pad it would destroy all of the rockets, mission control initiated the main ignition sequence and in a blaze of orange the damaged rocket fired up before slowly rising up. When the leaking fuel reached the blazing engines below, it ignited and the fire snaked up the side of the rocket. A few hundred yards from the ground, the fire reached the hole in the main tank and with a humungous, earth shaking explosion, the rocket exploded to bits. The brightness of the blast was so great and hot that even in the oppressive heat of the night, those charging the rockets bent over to cringe from the temperature, some actually hearing the crackling of their skin frying on their face.

A second main thruster was ignited and then a third as the two remaining rockets began to reach for the sky even as the hulk of the destroyed rocket faltered, and then crashed to Earth. Several of the attackers stopped to steady themselves and fire on the rocket, but the distance was too great and the rockets continued their rise. The tank, attacking at full speed, squeezed off a last round, but the distance combined with the accelerating movement and height the rockets had gained, allowed the shot to miss.

Inside the rocket ship some seats were tightly secured by the seatbelts, while others held two people – with a few even three – passengers. Those who couldn't reach a seat were clinging onto the seatbacks, the people in the seats, and anything else they could get their hands on. As the rockets continued to accelerate toward the sky, those not in seats began to fall to the back, slamming into the bottom with the crunches and snaps of bones breaking as quickly a heap of broken humans began to grow on the ground.

Having secured a seat in the main cabin of a surviving rocket, Senator Fillmore was now focused on the space station, saying, "Ah good. In a few minutes we will be free of Earth's pull. I understand that it will be less than an hour.

"Uh, no," said the Captain, "That would be if we lifted off on time. Unfortunately, we're on the wrong side of the Earth."

"Oh my. Is that a problem?"

"No, not really. We got booster rockets. Just need a different trajectory. That's all. That… and it will be longer."

"How long?"

"Couldn't say. Haven't done this before. We'll see."

Senator Fillmore wanted more details, but the Captain was so calm in his response, so cool. He decided not to worry about reaching the space station. Rather he would concentrate on the remaining passengers. Times of trouble were great for displaying compassion. That was a lesson he learned in his first term as Senator and never forgot. Once it was safe, and maybe even before, he would check on the remaining passengers. That was what made leaders… leading, or if not leading, giving the impression of leadership. He didn't get to be Senator Fillmore by just sitting about after all.

For Food and Water

Food and water. Can't live without it. Not a statement of great thought but rather a simple fact. If SS 222 was without either, or at least enough to make the three year trip, everyone would die. If there was a shortage of meals onboard, they'd have to order more and wait. What else could be done? Starve? After all, another fifteen hundred people were arriving and soon. In the case of Gordon Johnson, just having one meal late was a problem, and he was already hungry. But such information, it must be handled delicately. If word got out that there was a food or water shortage... panic might be the result. Everyone was edgy, complements of spending month after month on Earth as it slowly warmed up. It was much better that Gordon keep this potential disaster to himself until a better reading was completed. On the positive side, there were fifty thousand meals or more on board. Not bad... just not enough.

How much water was onboard? That was next on his list. Well, that and determining the number of empty food lockers. Returning to his family, the orders were simple orders. The children, Jon and Mia, were to search the half of the ship not yet passed through. Looking for... well, anything. Food, dirt, seeds, ovens, pillows, blankets, computers... anything other than molded steel. Of course that isn't how he explained the task. Instead they were told, "Check out the back and report back what you find." They were kids and had to be spoken to as such. He'd make a thorough search of the area himself once he had a chance. He loved his kids, but some things aren't to be left to children, that's why they are called children. They'd give him an idea what was in the back of the ship, and kept them out of his hair while he checked the water and talked with Terri.

Confident they were out of earshot, he said softly, "We got to check the rest of the food bins,"

"Check the food..."

"Shhh!!!!" admonished Gordon.

"Shhh yourself! I'm tired of you bossing. I think space has gone to your head."

Grabbing her by her upper arms and shaking Gordon hissed, "Shut up! Shut up and listen! There's no food!"

Initially Terri was even angrier at being grabbed so aggressively. But then the words began to sink in. "No food? We saw…"

"I checked some other bins, numbers two, one ninety nine, and two hundred."

"Well… that doesn't mean…"

"No? Go see the message in bin number two. Go on. See for yourself before you start sniping at me."

Terri stared at Gordon in surprise. She'd seen him lose his cool, but never like this. "If there's no food, we can get…"

"There is no food. Don't you understand? No food. We need to check the other bins."

"No food?"

"Check bin number two. Go on. I know you think I'm crazy, so check it. Read the note."

"Ok… what is the passcode?"

"SS002. It's the same for each bin. Start with 'SS' then add the number."

Terri floated to bin number two and punched in the code. Waiting politely for the three beeps she opened the door and disappeared inside. Deciding not to wait, Gordon moved to bin three, punching in the code. Opening the door he was met with a barren light and empty space. As he closed the door he heard Terri say, "So they left a message. So what?"

"Three is empty."

"And?"

"And we need to check the rest. Hurry up. You work your way up and I'll go the other way. We'll meet on the other side."

Gordon didn't wait for an answer, instead pushing his feet against the wall as if in a pool, gliding over to number one ninety eight. Terri hesitated for a moment. She wanted to argue, if for no other reason than she didn't care for Gordon's attitude. But when he began to furiously punch in his code, she could see it was pointless. When Gordon was like this, there was nothing to be done. What was the big deal? If there was no food, they'd order more. Gordon didn't know Senator Fillmore like she did. He could make miracles happen, she'd seen it happen. Moving to bin number four, she punched in "SS004" and pulled the door open. Empty.

Continuing on, she was confronted with one empty bin after another. At first the task was disappointing, then depressing. Finally, as she opened the last few doors she began to softly cry. As Gordon closed the door to the last bin she said softly, "Gordon, what are we going to do?"

Trying to ignore her, he said, "First, we'll see if we have water. No water and we have to get another rocket ship up here somehow." He knew that if he tried to cheer her up, she'd only descend further into worrying about their plight.

"And if we have water?"

"Hmmm… don't know. Let's see how much we have first. Come on, help me."

Gordon traveled back to food bin number one, turning the levers to release a hatch on the ceiling before pulling it open. The entire ship was cordoned off into sealed areas. With such a big craft, there was a good possibility a random space rock might puncture the hull. If that happened, each area of the ship could be sealed in an instant. Clicking the small flashlight that came with the clipboard, Gordon dove into the darkness above, disappearing from sight. As Terri looked up she could see the dim glow of the flashlight floating about like a moth. Then she heard some metallic clangs as Gordon banged against one of the tanks.

Problem was, how to determine if there was water inside without opening the tank. After all, if the water got out, that could be disaster. He tapped the flashlight on the outside of a water tank. The sound it made gave the impression water was inside, or so he guessed. But he couldn't be sure. Moving along the surface of the tank like a scuba diver, he used his hands to move about with the flashlight clenched between his teeth. Occasionally he'd kick a foot or swim a hand. Finally he found the latch.

Should he open it? Was it pressurized? He thought so. Finally he made the decision, they had to know. Turning the wheel attached to the door, it fought him at first before releasing with a "Klunk!" and water gushed out. Panicking, Gordon tried futilely to close the door as water exploded out. Finally he grabbed the metal u shaped handle welded onto the tank and Slammed the door closed, turning the wheel tight. They had water. This huge tank was big enough to hold sixty thousand gallons and was one of four. If the others were full, then they had almost a quarter million gallons.

Estimating each person needed a gallon of water a day, that would be almost one hundred days or three months of water, not enough for the trip on its own. But then one had to consider the spaceship was self contained and sealed. That meant that every drop of water would be used either for drinking or the garden. Water expelled in the bathroom was collected in the ship's sanitation plant where it would separate and purify the water, returning it to the tanks, while the solids were transferred to the garden as fertilizer. The ship even had evaporators installed in the air conditioning units to pull excess water from the air. If they managed it properly, they could arrive at New Earth with as much water as currently held in the tanks. That was the theory anyway.

They had water, but were all four tanks full? Gordon moved to the next tank and turned the wheel. But this time he was more careful, grabbing the handle next to the hatch. As it started to pop open, he pushed it closed, losing only a few gallons for his effort. With globules of water floating about him, the last two tanks were checked. Sure enough, full as well. Turning back to the square of light that represented a return to Terri and the food bins Gordon smiled grimly. Fifty thousand meals and plenty of water. Could they survive three years on that?

As soon as he popped his head through the opening to the food bin aisle Terri asked, "Water?"

"Yup. All kinds. Tanks are full."

"Yea!"

"Yea!" said Gordon cheerfully and with a playful tone. "So what now?"

Staring down the corridor as the sounds of Jon and Mia returning, he asked, "Find anything?"

"Nope," said Mia.

"And you Jon?"

"Naw. Some guys took some dumps on the floors, that's it."

"Jon!"

"Sorry ma, but that's all I found."

"Ok, knock it off Jon. We get it."

"But pop, they did. Then smeared some words in it."

"Jon!" said Terri.

"Don't worry. I won't say what. I guess they were upset they didn't get to go along."

"Ok Jon, and no, we don't need to know what they said. So Gordon, what's next?"

"Hmmm… I guess, let's see the Captain. He should be in the wheelhouse. That's where the main computer is. We better have that."

"The bridge," said Jon.

"What?"

"Com on Pop, wheelhouse? Really? They have Star Trek when you were a kid? Wheelhouse… that's for a boat on a river."

Gordon frowned at his mouthy son. He had two problems with Jon's talk. One, he felt it was disrespectful, and two… quite frankly the kid's mind was quicker than his.

"You know what?" said Jon with a mock serious stare at Gordon, "We might have to Captain Kirk-il-ize you. Cause right now, you're just sad."

Godron's jaw clenched as he wished he had something even cleverer to reply with, but he only got out a threatening, "How bout I…" before he was interrupted.

"And then food?" asked Mia hopefully, wanting to defuse the situation.

Smiling at her after one last glare of death at Jon, Gordon said, "Yeah, sure. I hope so. And then some food."

Knowing how upset Gordon's could get when hungry, Terri added, "Yes… food. Something to improve your father's mood."

Jon chuckled before adding, "Yeah, that will make it so much easier for me when I Captain Kirk-il-ize you. Or no… wait, I'll have you Spock-ed."

"Shut up Jon!" snapped Gordon.

Jon giggled. Yes, Gordon was hungry.

Anchors Aweigh!

The bridge was located at the front of the ship with a checkerboard of four small windows imbedded in the front facing, and four more on the sides. Through these windows the vast expanse of space was on display. When Gordon and Terri entered, Jon and Mia were left behind to keep the conversation private. This was sensitive information the children didn't need to know. As far as Gordon was concerned, the phrase, "Loose lips sink ships," was extremely accurate right now. The Captain offered no greeting as they entered, too occupied with staring at his computer screen. There was an audio playing along with what he was watching, too soft to understand, sounding like some sort of argument. Not surprising, that was mostly what was shown on television these days. As he approached, Gordon noted the Captain's youthful appearance, but for someone so young he appeared rather grim, and the wrinkles added a bit of maturity to his face.

Glancing up from his screen, the Captain's mind was elsewhere as Gordon stopped a respectful distance away saying, "Captain, Gordon Johnson. Structural engineer."

Acting confused the Captain extended a hand saying, "Um yes. Nice to meet you."

"Yes sir. We need to talk. Terri, close the door."

"Please!" demanded Terri.

"A… sure. Would you *please* close the door."

Frowning at Gordon as she passed by, Gordon said, "This is serious, very serious. Is there anyone else who we need to include? I'd like to keep this to a minimum."

"Hmmm… yeah. Um, why don't you tell me what you have, and we'll take it from there."

"As I'm sure you know, my first responsibility was to check the ship from stem to stern for anything that might cause concern to delay our departure."

The Captain's confused look indicated that he was anything but aware of this, but still nodded as if he knew.

"While I am happy to report that the ship is in fact in excellent shape, there are other issues that need to be addressed and immediately."

"Go on."

Gordon glanced around as if there might be someone else in the sparse bridge.

"Don't worry Gordon, we are alone."

Gordon nodded, but still hesitated before continuing with, "We can make a more detailed check of things… and I think we should, but it appears much of the supplies didn't make it on board. Pillows, personal computers, and other things."

Again the Captain nodded, saying, "Yes, well at this point, what can be done? Why don't you put together a larger detail and make a more thorough search. I mean either it is or isn't here… yes? Nothing we can make a fuss about now."

Gordon chewed his lips, not wanting to say more. But he had to. There was no other way about it. "Food."

"Food? Yes, what about it?"

"We are supposed to have two hundred food bins, filled all the way."

"Yes, but if one or two are low. Not a problem. You weren't to know this, but we have a limited passenger. Missing a few carrots and beans is manageable."

Gordon paused until Terri touched him softly on the lower back, her way of saying to continue. "I'm not talking about a few carrots and beans."

"Well… what then is it?"

"It's… well it's not the water. Even though I wasn't supposed to, I checked the water tanks. Full to the brim thank god."

"Yes, that is good. And remember, we have the gardens. You likely forgot that."

"No, I included the gardens. In fact, there aren't any."

"What? No gardens? Why that simply isn't so. Huge ones in fact. Pillows, yes I'm not surprised. Those types of things are forgot, all the time. But you must be mistaken. We need gardens, as a backup if nothing else. Check the back of the ship. That's where the excess passengers we won't be carrying would have been put up. They likely dumped the dirt there. Oh, and the seeds. Mustn't forget them. That definitely needs to be found."

"Checked already, and I'll check again, but don't think I would miss huge piles of dirt."

"Well check again."

"That's only part of the problem."

"What's that?"

"We've a bigger one."

"Yes, and that is?"

"Food."

"Yes. You said a few bins are a bit short."

"No, you did. I didn't say any such thing."

Showing a flash of anger, the Captain said, "Well then, what did you say?"

"It isn't what I said, but what I didn't."

"And that is?"

"Food, there is none, or very little."

"What?! We have two hundred bins... what did you find when you checked them?"

"How did you know that?"

"I could see on the main computer, showed you were opening the bins. You weren't supposed to. I was going to shut you out."

"Why?"

"I used to work in restaurants, you know the main cause of restaurants going under?"

"No."

"Theft. Theft of food. Imagine if that were to happen here. I was this close to changing the passwords and locking you out."

"Don't bother now. There is no food."

"None?"

"Hardly. Out of two hundred bins… one."

"One out of what?"

"One of two hundred."

"Opened every one of them. Nothing."

"That can't be."

"It is. You could see us on your screen."

The Captain paused, then mumbled while trying to take in the meaning of Gordon's words. "Yes. It has a schematic of the food area, blinked when you entered each one. Only one full?"

"Yup."

"Why that means… I wonder how many meals that is."

"Bout fifty thousand."

"What? You sure?"

The Captain was drifting away, staring off into space, his brow scrunched up in thought.

"Captain. Captain! Don't you see? You've got to order more food. Why I'd guess one rocket filled up would do the trick."

Spinning toward Gordon and Terri, the Captain said, "No."

Terri tapped Gordon on the side with the back of her wrist. When Gordon finally looked over she shook her head as if to say the Captain seemed to be losing his mind. "Captain," she said, "I know Senator Fillmore. He'll get the food on board, but you must act, and now. Before he leaves. He can take care of it. He's a miracle worker. You've no idea."

Turning to face Terri the Captain said, "No. You've no idea. I've been monitoring the situation on Earth. You've no idea."

"What?" asked Gordon, "What is it?"

"Chaos."

"Chaos? What's that supposed to mean?"

"It means the tear on the bottom of the Pacific Ocean has expanded greatly, temperatures have shot up... over two hundred by now. Do you understand?"

"Why that's all the more reason."

"No, it's not. As I said, you've no idea. The remaining rockets XJ1, 2, and 3. Had to take off. Emergency, or so the reports are. Some nuts claim to have shot one down with a tank."

"A tank? Are you crazy?"

"No. I'm not. You think we can find someone to fill up a rocket ship with food and shoot it off to us in that kind of atmosphere?"

"Well... why not? We've got empty space. Payment for passage. Even enough for another few bins, and maybe some dirt and seeds."

"Don't think so. The report is, those with the tank aren't alone. Masses of people have swamped the remaining few rocket ships. Anarchy, total and complete. Murder, you name it, and why not. If you were in a two hundred and fifty degree oven, wouldn't you do anything to get out?"

"Yes but," said Terri, "Senator Fillmore. He can do anything."

"I'm sure he can. And would you like to know what he sent us just before he took off? Apparently he has taken on extra passengers and wants to switch out some people on board for the excess. He doesn't know that I... rather what we now know."

"Why, what did he do?"

"He made a list of passengers. Those who were to be cordoned off and kept away from everyone else. Once they dock, he wants them put on board the rocket and returned to earth. Your last name... Johnson?"

"Yes, why?"

"Cause a Terri, Gordon, Mia, and Jon Johnson are all on the list."

Terri blanched at the comment. "Back on the rocket? You've got to be kidding."

"We aren't going anywhere," announced Gordon.

The comments made little impression on the Captain, who replied calmly, "They have guns. Trust me, I'm sure lots of them. It seems in the final hours before liftoff there was a full fledged war going on around the launch pad. I'm guessing they have a small army on those rockets now. And they've gotten used to shooting them at other people. I tell you it's crazy down there. Might be up here as well."

"Well," muttered Gordon without much conviction, "We ain't going."

Surprisingly the Captain appeared to agree, saying, "Don't blame you. I wouldn't want to go either."

"So you'll back us?"

"Sure, I'd love to. But like I say. They got guns." It was odd. The way the Captain said it, as if bothered the Johnsons were being thrown off... determined to keep the current passengers on board the spacecraft.

"So Captain, what do we do?"

"Well, first of all. You said fifty thousand meals?"

"Yeah."

"Did you count them?"

"What? Count fifty thousand meals. You know how long that will take?"

"Yeah. Is it box meals?"

"Looked like it."

"You're a structural engineer. Figure it out. Count a small section and then multiply. If one one hundredth is a thousand, then the whole is a hundred thousand. Got it? We don't need a count to the unit, but I need a good idea."

"Why?" asked Terri, "We already know how much is in a bin. I saw the specs. Gordon's right. It's fifty thousand."

The Captain became irritated, saying, "We got two ships coming at us… like rocket ships. Literally, and loaded with guns. You two check the food bin and I'll make a sweep of the back of the ship. Anyone else know?"

"No."

"Your kids?"

"No."

"Hmmm… Ok. How long before you can do that? After all, we got hungry people on board."

"What does that matter?"

"They're going to want to eat and soon."

"Can't we give them a snack?"

The Captain frowned as if Gordon said something very stupid. "No. Not yet. They get nothing. Nothing at all… for now. We got a thousand people on board. How fast can you check the food? Fifteen minutes?"

"Well now. That might be a little fast. I could only see the first couple of rows of food. Who knows what else is in there. Half hour is reasonable."

The Captain was furiously punching the keyboard to the computer. Then he said, "Ok, that's it. But make it fifteen. I've changed the passwords to the food bins. They are now "xyz" and the bin number. So bin number one the password is, "xyz001" and so on. Got it?"

"Yeah," said Terri, "Sure, 'xyz001' not a problem."

Pushing himself toward the door in the weightless environment the Captain said, "Ok, let's go."

Gordon got the sense more was going on than a simple count of meals. The Captain acted as if on a mission to accomplish something, but what?

"Captain," said Gordon, "Something wrong?"

"You'll see," said the Captain with a frown, "Just give me a count of how many meals I got."

10000 Meals

As they silently pushed along the corridors toward the food bins, the Captain, Gordon, and Terri looked like a small school of fish on the hunt, darting back and forth in the hallway from side to side as if searching the nooks and crannies for bits of food. As they approached the food bins voices could be heard complaining.

Turning the corner to food bin 001, two men were standing in front of it, one with a ruddy fat face, and the other thin with a pencil moustache to match.

"It's not working," complained the thin man.

"Punch it in again," said the fat man, his face now just a touch redder.

"Can I help you?" asked Gordon.

The thin man jumped at the words, but the fat man turned with a scowl. "We're here to get some food."

"That's not possible," said the Captain.

"Oh yes it is. The Admiral sent us."

The Captain hesitated, but only for a moment. "Well, when he takes the con, he makes the decision. But right now we're in dock. Get it?"

"No I don't."

"Until we head out and the initial check is made, I'm in charge. Not you. Not your friend there. And not the Admiral. How's that do."

"Well, we got hungry people."

"The code doesn't work," complained the thin man again.

Ignoring the grumpy fat man, the Captain glared at the thin man saying, "I know. Because you triggered an alarm on the bridge. Someone was breaking into the food bin."

"We weren't breaking in," objected the fat man, "We're the chefs, I worked personally at Chez Inez, was hired on here by Senator Fillmore, and we got orders…"

"No!" snarled the Captain, "I don't know who you are, and quite frankly I don't care." Then pointing at Gordon he said, "We came down here to investigate a break in at food bin 001. Now, unless you want my head of security here to lock you up, I suggest you go back to the dining rooms where you belong... got it?"

The fat man glanced over at Gordon, who was not a small man and looked fairly healthy. Certainly the fat man was bigger – much bigger – but his girth seemed more to do with eating than muscle development. Finally he backed down, mumbling angrily, "We got orders."

"And I'm giving you new ones. Go back to where you belong. The dining room and... Mr. Head of Security.

"Um... yeah?" said Gordon.

"If you see these two or any others around the food bin, arrest them! And if they resist, use all force necessary. Got it?"

"Yes, all force necessary," said Gordon with authority.

"And now gentlemen... beat it before I change my mind."

The fat man pursed his lips in a silent last protest before pushing off toward the dining room, the thin man tailing dutifully behind.

The Captain watched until the men were out of sight before saying quietly, "That was close. Both of you, hurry up. This is getting worse by the minute." Then he pushed toward the back of the ship, disappearing into the dimly lit hallway.

"What was the code?" asked Gordon.

"I got it," said Terri, her delicate fingers tapping the keypad. Three beeps and a green light later Gordon grabbed the latch and opened the door. Again there was a slight whoosh of cold air as the stacks of frozen meals came into view, filling the space all the way to the top of the ceiling.

"How we going to do this?" asked Terri.

"Simple, like the Captain said, count a little bit and multiply. First let's pull some of this out of here, make an alleyway. That'll give us a better feel for how deep the cooler really is." As he spoke Gordon grabbed a stack of frozen meals in the middle on top, lowering them down and handing them to Terri. "Here, stack them over there and I'll keep going. With the ship in weightless mode, it was seconds before a small section of meals had been removed, maybe two feet wide and a two feet deep. "Looks good so far," said Gordon, "Ok, the opening's about five feet wide. What do you think Terri?"

She placed her arms wide touching one of the walls. "Yup, we took out about two by two, the room looks five feet wide." Then she stretched her arms out. "Yeah. Five feet I'd guess."

"How tall you figure?"

"Oh I don't know, nine, maybe ten feet."

"Yeah, I'd say that, let's use ten, easier math. Doesn't matter though if it's stacked this way all the way to the back. But good to know anyway. Leave what we took out to one side and we'll count that. Once we get the depth, simple math. Captain was right."

Again Gordon reached up high to grab some meals, but as he pushed against the tray of food something strange happened. The stack of meals began to float toward the back of the food bin.

"What the hell?" said Gordon.

Peeking through the doorway Terri asked, "Gordon? You alright?"

"Shit!"

Pulling herself through the door she said, "What's wrong? What's... oh my." She could see through the hallway created that the first three feet of storage were stuffed with frozen foods... after that food bin number one was like all the others. Empty. There were no fifty thousand meals on board. Nothing like it. One thousand passengers for three years... and they had to live on three feet of food. How was that going to happen?

Gordon, seeming nervous, said, "We gotta get this food back inside," as he pushed for the back of the room. Then turning around and putting his heels against the wall he began to pace as best he could forward in the gravityless ship while counting quietly, "One... two... three... four... five." He stopped there with his toes on the edge of the meals that were in the front of the bin. Then with one last step he said, "Five. Say three feet to a step."

Grabbing the sides of the door he said to Terri, "Five paces, fifteen feet. And one pace worth of food, or three feet. You sure these hold a fifty thousand meals?"

"Yes... actually a little more. Maybe just under a fifty five thousand. It's been a while since I saw the plans."

"Ok, we got twenty percent of that. Say... ten thousand meals."

The conversation stopped as voices could be heard, loud and angry, approaching.

"Come on," said Gordon, "Get these meals inside."

Terri neatly began to pick up a palate of food when Gordon snatched it from her, tossing it inside saying, "Hurry, no one can see this."

As the voices approached Gordon and Terri furiously tossed the trays into the food bin, sending the meals floating inside. As the last trays disappeared and the door closed, three men appeared around the corner.

"Open that door!" ordered one of the men. The fat chef was beside a man with steel white hair, a wrinkled face, and a frown on his face. Behind them the thin chef trailed meekly behind.

"I am Admiral Pitts! And I want food served!"

"Yes Admiral," said Terri smartly, I recognize you, I'm Terri Johnson, on staff with Senator Fillmore."

"I don't give a damn if your God himself! Open this door!"

"Can't."

"What do you mean?"

"The code has changed. We can't get in."

"Code changed?" said the fat chef, "You don't have it?"

"No. Neither does Gordon here."

"Then what the hell are you doing here?" raged the old man.

"To keep everyone else from the food," said Gordon, using his most commanding voice.

"And I want it open!"

"And you are?"

"I just told you, you idiot! Admiral Pitts!"

"Admiral?"

"Yes, Admiral. And I am in charge of this ship."

"You are? Right now?"

"What does that mean?"

"Simply this, we are in pre-check. During that time until the structural integrity is verified and the equipment check completed and signed off on, you... *Admiral*, are not in charge."

The Admiral sneered in frustration as the fat chef shouted, "Nonsense! You open this door!"

Staring with malice at Gordon the Admiral said in a low voice, "No, he's right. But let me ask you this... what was your name?"

"Gordon," sneered Gordon.

"Gordon," the Admiral sneered back, "Soon I am going to be running this ship, under the authority of Senator Fillmore. Do you really want to go down this path? Think about it. We will be in deep space in a short period of time, then on a new planet. You really want me as your enemy?"

"No, but we aren't in deep space, and you aren't in charge. I was told to watch the food bins for poachers. That's my job Admiral. Are you asking me to quit my post?"

The Admiral frowned even deeper, but inside his sense of order and duty began to assert itself. "No," he said gruffly.

"Then I'm going to have to ask you to return to the dining room."

The Admiral glared at Gordon a moment, and then snarled, "Come on, let's go."

"But..." blustered the fat chef.

"Shut up! He's right. But so am I, soon I'll be running things here, and there will be new orders given. We'll see how he likes following then." The comment earned a few guffaws from the fat chef and even a greedy titter from the thin chef.

As the men's voices disappeared down the hallway toward the dining room, the Captain came up behind Gordon, peering nervously over Terri's shoulder. The Captain asked in a soft voice, "Well?"

"Bad news."

"What's that?"

"Ten Thousand."

"Meals? And that's all?"

"Yup."

"I got worse," said the Captain.

"That is?"

"No dirt, seeds. Nothing. Just empty rooms."

"What are we going to do," asked Terri.

With a grim determination the Captain said, "First to the bridge. Get your kids and don't talk to anyone. I mean it. Grab them and go. You didn't send them to the dining rooms did you?"

"No. They're away from everyone. And then?"

"And then we'll see if you understand what is going on. Gordon, you pretty good in math?"

"Yup, kind of a job requirement for an engineer."

"Good. This should be rather quick. Has to be. After all, we don't know when Senator Fillmore will be arriving."

Thoughts On Mankind, Life, And Death

As the Captain began speaking, his bearing had all the seriousness of a leader. Brow furrowed, lips pulled tight, and steely eyes darting at his audience. "Ten thousand meals," he said gravely, "Ten thousand meals. You know the length of our voyage?"

"Three years... pretty much." said Terri.

"Exactly. How long you think that's going to last?"

"Well," mumbled Gordon. He hadn't really thought of it that way. He was so concerned about finding everything he never ran the numbers. "Guess it's going to be tight."

"No, it's not," replied the Captain, "Not for everyone."

Terri, glanced nervously at the Captain, then Gordon. Almost immediately she became visibly upset, as if about to become ill saying, "You're not..."

"What?" asked Gordon, clearly confused.

"Gordon," said the Captain, "The numbers, work the numbers. Ten thousand meals... a thousand people."

Gordon scrunched his face as he prepared to work out the problem, but almost immediately his eyes popped open wide as he said, "Ten meals. Ten meals per person."

"No," said Terri with determination, "We can't do that."

Turning to Terri the Captain said, "Ten thousand meals, three year trip – minimum. Think about it. We eat three meals a day, that's a thousand per year. Three years – that's three thousand meals. That mean's we got little more than enough food for three people."

Looking stunned, Gordon said, "I never thought of that. Why, that's just enough for us in this room."

"Yup," agreed the Captain, "Throw your kids in and were all covered."

"So you want to what? Kill everyone else?" Terri was now shaking slightly.

"Enough for five. Say ten if we stretch it. Maybe... maybe fifteen if we starve."

"But... that's murder."

"What do you call taking everyone on? We all live for now, and then die in how long? We are the lucky ones. Right here and now we are the ones who get to choose who lives and dies. And therefore we can live."

"But I can't do that."

"What do you think Admiral Pitts would do? You want me to call him in here?"

Staring at the floor Terri said in a murmur, "No."

"Good. I hate to speak plainly, but it is what it is. We've no time for sentimentality."

"Well I care," Terri said angrily.

"And so do I. But right now we've got to put a number on how many survive. Is it us? Just five, or ten? What is the number, and remember, if were wrong, we can all die."

Gordon had only half been listening to the conversation, or so it seemed. "We can do more."

Getting slightly angry, the Captain said, "Did you not hear me? Unless you know of some food that I'm not aware of, we got ten thousand meals. That's it. No time to play games. If the Senator boards. We are all in trouble."

"There's more food."

"More food? Where?"

"Donner."

After a brief silence, Terri said, "Oh really Gordon... don't go there."

"It's that, or they're all dead, or almost so."

"Donner... what's that?" asked the Captain.

"The Donner party," said Terri, "Back in the days of the old west. Trying to get to California, got stuck in the Rocky Mountains from the snow... there all winter. When they ran out of food, they ate the ones who died."

"See," said Gordon, "It's been done before."

"Yes," snapped Terri, "They ate the ones who died. They didn't pick who would live."

"No," said Gordon with slight irritation, "But that was different. We can choose who can live for a reason. We already know the food is gone. We already know it will be three years minimum before we get more. We'll be in deep space. No oasis or wayside that serves up cold drinks and burgers."

"I know that."

"Well then, the Captain's right. We can choose who lives. The better we choose, the more will live."

A quiet came over the room as the three considered their conversation. The Captain said, "Gordon, you're right. We can do more than fifteen. Donner it is so to speak. So now, it's a matter of who. But first how many."

"How many indeed."

"No! It's everyone. When someone dies, then we can... oh god, I can't even say it."

"That's all right Terri," consoled Gordon, "But if we do it your way, when someone dies, everyone will be exhausted and worn out. We'd start starving in a week or less. Let's make the choice now. That's the healthiest, and smartest way about it. Remember, we don't know what this new planet is going to be like. Could be full of food, or almost empty."

"Yes," said Terri hopefully, "Full of food."

"But," said the Captain, "We don't know. We can't make the easiest decision, it has to be the best. For all we know this could decide the fate of humanity."

"No, I don't want to."

Glancing from Gordon to Terri and back, the Captain continued, "Ok. This is how it will work. As of right now, we are the Supreme Counsel. We take votes on everything. And, as of right now, the vote is the Donner issue. Are we to select who lives and dies?" The Captain paused to let his words sink in. "All in favor of the Donner option, raise your hand." Both Gordon and the Captain lifted a hand. "That settles it."

"I don't like this," grumbled Terri.

Trying to sound upbeat, the Captain said, "Ok. Duly noted. One strong objection. On to the next order of business. How many?"

"I'm guessing two hundred," said Gordon.

"Two hundred? How'd you get that?"

"That's four people per person. I don't know how much is on a person, say a hundred pounds. Figure a hundred pounds per year, plus a year's worth once we land."

"Oh my god Gordon, I never thought I'd married such a man."

"Damn it Terri, the Captain's right. I've heard you talk about some of the planets we're shipping people off to. No hope in hell. One is a fireball… literally. Those are your words. We have no idea what we are going to find when we land. We can't land exhausted and find out we've got two years of work to save our lives… to save humanity. Tell me I'm wrong."

"No, you're right. It's true. But do we need that much food?"

"Well. A hundred pounds average. That's not even a third of a pound per day. Little more than a quarter pounder every day, no fries or anything else. No snacks. Just water."

"A hundred pounds sounds a little light."

"Maybe, but even at a hundred fifty, that's not even a half pound a day."

Nodding in agreement the Captain said, "We've got to move along. As I said, if the others get on board, either we become the food… or shipped back to Earth. Are we in agreement? Two hundred?"

"Yes," said Gordon firmly while Terri could only nod her head.

"Good! Now the next is who."

"The kids," said Gordon.

"Yes, I agree. The children. Why, they are smaller… will eat less."

"And the others are bigger, more to eat," said Terri softly, frowning even as she spoke the words.

"Are you alright?" asked Gordon.

"Yes. We've no time. I'll deal with this later. That's Ok. Let's keep moving."

Pushing away from the wall the Captain glided over the keyboard for the computer saying , "We've got the passenger listing. Doesn't give weight, but has the ages."

"Great," said Gordon shoving himself over as well. "Can you sort it?"

"Think so."

Terri slid over as the Captain clacked away at the keyboard, finally saying, "There. Got it. So what is the cut off? Ten?"

"How about fourteen?" offered Gordon, "How many is that?"

"Hmmm… One hundred seventy five."

"Can we go older?" asked Terri.

"That leaves only twenty five adults. Let's face it. That's a lot of unsupervised children. Many without parents."

"Oh god."

"What?" asked Gordon.

"We're going to ask children… children to eat the parents we killed."

Gordon bit his lip before saying, "No. We can monitor that."

"Does that make all this any better? Killing their parents? You feel better now?"

"Yes," said the Captain bluntly, hoping to make it easier for Gordon to deal with his wife, "We are going to survive. And if that means killing the parents to save the children, then so be it. I'd advise you to start thinking that way. *Positive*. What we are doing is making the best out of a bad situation. I can think of a hundred ways this becomes much worse. So let's keep it upbeat."

Nodding weakly with a tear in her eye, Terri sniffed before saying, "Yes. I suppose you're right. I'll do my best."

"Good. Let's start with that. One hundred seventy five children. That covers everyone fourteen and under. We can always raise or lower the number if we need to. Now its time for the other twenty five. Who do we need to run this ship? And who do we want to survive. And by that I mean, once we land, we need to build a community. You might not want to hear this, but I don't want to live in a city of dishwashers and maids. I want more. And given the choices available, I say we take advantage."

"And how can we do that?" asked Gordon.

"Passenger register. Everyone is in it, and covers everyone's education and job title. Your Senator Fillmore is quite detailed if nothing else."

"That's all?"

"Well, we don't have time for interviews now do we?"

"Guess not. How many to pick from?"

"About eight hundred twenty. I hate to say it, but the younger the better. Likely it's going to be hard living, and not just on board, but once we land. A seventy year old isn't going to do nearly as much as a twenty five year old."

"Agreed, and as many women as men," stated Terri emphatically.

"What?"

"Well dear, think of it. If not then either I am to become New Earth's whore, or I'll take on several other husbands. You don't want that do you?"

Despite the grim subject, Gordon managed a chuckle. "No, guess not. We'll try at least."

The Captain managed a laugh as well. This was ghoulish stuff, a little of humor was appreciated.

The Adults Left Standing

So who was it to be? Eight hundred twenty adults, young adults, and teenagers. And only twenty five slots. About three for every hundred onboard, and decisions had to be made quickly. No one knew how much time they had before Senator Fillmore arrived – with his guns. At least that was Terri's opinion. The Captain had so far been accommodating to Terri and Gordon, but people change their mind with the circumstances. A large group of men with guns could easily sway the Captain to change his position. That meant the Senator's arrival could be a death sentence for the Johnson family. No doubt, Terri was still shaken by the gruesome decisions being made, but the innate sense to protect her family was taking control – the desire to survive making everything easier.

The shaking was gone, as were the misty eyes. Make no mistake, she'd cry later, but for now, Terri had her game face on. While working for Senator Fillmore, she was listed as an Administrative Aide. But Terri, with her quick mind and natural determination, had proved herself to be much more than that. That's how she got her family onboard. Sure, Gordon qualified as a structural engineer, kind of. Technically his background was a mechanical engineering degree. Close enough, or so thought Senator Fillmore after some lobbying by Terri, when choosing the passenger list. At least close enough to select him as one of the peons that would make his life easier on New Earth. And now as she scanned the passenger list, her eyes darting back and forth, it was with the same cold hearted and ruthless attitude that had kept others off the ship to make room for her family. When she initially discovered her selection for passage on SS 222, Terri had personally sought out Senator Fillmore and cried genuine tears as she thanked him. But now things were different. Survival dictated such behavior.

Almost at the top of the list was Admiral Pitts, whom she had met twice and found distasteful on both occasions. He was one of the many reptile like personalities Senator Fillmore kept close to consolidate and keep his power. One of the many disreputable folks the Senator joked about as being his, "Personal assassins."

The next name her eyes stopped on was Senator Fillmore. It was unspoken but obvious. The Senator would not be allowed on SS 222 under any circumstances. With this bond broken, so too was any loyalty she held for the Senator's lackeys. There were three women on the listing. All young – or fairly so, pretty, and marked for death. They were the Senator's private harem of girlfriends. Women Terri was sure the Senator's wife knew about but did nothing to stop. He was a Senator after all. Full of lipstick, makeup, and catty conversation. Snotty and rude were there calling cards, and Terri would be damned if she'd spend the rest of her life with them. Not if she had the choice.

Scanning the list, Admiral Pitts was first to be addressed. In the detailed passenger register, his line showed graduation from Annapolis – third in his class. Forty years service in the Navy, reaching the rank of Rear Admiral, lowest of the Admiral's ranks. For the last ten years he had been a lobbyist for a large weapons manufacturer, using old Navy relationships to earn new contracts. Something he was very well paid for. Seventy four years old. Terri couldn't think of a single reason to keep the elderly, obnoxious, jerk on board. Now positioned as an enemy of Senator Fillmore, she could see the value of such a man. Once relocated on New Earth, he would likely be in charge of the newly created police force and army. Loyal beyond a fault to the Senator, she saw him as the leader of a fascist organization that would keep all opposition intimidated.

Facing the Captain, she said, "Admiral Pitts… any reason we need to keep him?"

Seeming a little nervous at the name, the Captain said, "Um, no. He's Admiral only in title. A spaceship isn't anything like a ship on the ocean. And its been god knows how long since he's been in command. In short, we don't need him."

"I don't think we need him otherwise," said Terri, a touch of venom in her voice. Gordon, who had been married for some time now, glanced slyly over at her. It was easy to pick out the change in her voice. She'd be fine now, or until all this settled down. Then of course there would be months of remorse. Tears in the middle of the night as well as day, constant private conversations about what she had done. And that was alright. Especially since she was in the proper frame of mind for now. They were going to need all of it right now.

"Who's going to fly this ship?"

Clearing his throat, the Captain said, "Why me of course."

For the first time Terri took in the tall skinny man before her. Young, definitely so. Intelligent, he'd proven that. Decisive and caring. All good traits for a Captain. But young, very young. And that was odd. The Senator liked his troops on the seasoned side. He was often quoting phrases such as, "I want someone with a track record. Don't give me promise or theories. I want someone who's been there and done that. Someone I can trust, and know what he's going to do when the shit comes down." There was no concept of being too old for Senator Fillmore. But too young?

She couldn't remember any of the Senator's inner circle that could be described as young. In fact that was a criticism of the Senator, that he was out of touch with modern day society. Unaware of what people thought and how they behaved. No she concluded, he would never select this young man, no matter the promise or intelligence. Could he have been selected by others for the Senator? Possibly Admiral Pitts? No, not a chance. Someone else then?

Narrowing her eyes to slits she said, "What exactly is your name and title?"

Suddenly nervous, the Captain began to sweat. "My name, why its... um."

"Never mind, it'll show on the register." Scrolling down the listing, she came across the following.

Vern Lipscomb: School – Annapolis, first in class;
Employment – Twenty Years Navy. Age – 58; SS 222
Assignment – Captain.

Glaring at the Captain she said, "Mighty young to be
fifty eight, wouldn't you say… Vern?"
"What's that?"
"Ok, Captain, what's your name?"
"My name? Why you know…"
Again scrolling down the page she reached the lower
twenties, and was shocked to see the following.

Brian Majewski: School – Annapolis, twenty third in
class; Employment – Five Years Navy; Age – 23; SS 222
Assignment - Sub-lieutenant.

"You're twenty three? Twenty three?"
"Yes… that's correct."
"Why didn't you say so when we came on the bridge,"
thundered Gordon.
"You didn't ask."
"And when you were addressed as Captain?"
"I did what was necessary. Would you rather be
dealing with Admiral Pitts? Or how about Captain
Lipscomb? I saw you stop on his name. You know Admiral
Pitts? Then you've met Lipscomb - yes. He is the Admiral's
right hand man. Has been for some time."

Terri's anger was gone, now replaced with an unhappy memories. She knew Lipscomb. Even for a woman who didn't believe in swearing, she would describe Lipscomb as a cruel bastard. Nasty in conversation. Treated women like dirt, with a snide joke or a hard slap on the behind always possible. Huge, as in muscular, something he always tried to use to his advantage. Leaning over, invading peoples personal space. Intimidation was his calling card, something Admiral Pitts relished.

"Between you and the Captain, who can fly this ship?"

"No one. Just two Ensigns below me. That's the list. The rest are maintenance and the like. Think there's more on XJ1... the Senator's rocket."

Gordon looked at Terri. He always trusted her instincts, at least when she was in tigress mode. He could see her thinking, eyes fluttering, mouth slightly open with the tongue tapping the teeth. Finally she said, "Do you need two ensigns to assist, or is one enough?"

She had made the decision. Brian Majewski would be Captain. No vote, but then none was necessary, was there? She was one vote, and certainly Brian was the second. That was enough. But then she knew, when in her zone Gordon gave her a wide berth. She continued on, "Which one?"

Wanting to move on from his informal promotion, Captain Majewski said, "Ensign Beers."

"Beers? I hope that isn't an indication of his behavior."

"Don't think so. But let's be honest. If I die or otherwise incapacitated, he's got the snap to take my place. That is if I train him."

"I would hope so. What else we need?"

There were two screens on the Bridge and Gordon had pulled up the list on the second. He said, "First of all. We got three infants, under a year. I say the parents go with them. Any objections?"

"What do they do?" asked the Captain.

"Um, one a kitchen helper, another is registered nurse, and… the third woman has a degree in computers. As for the men… a lawyer, financial planner, and accountant."

"I'm good with those."

"Pretty easy to please Captain," said Terri.

"Yup. Got guns coming. The sooner we depart, the better. And we need all of those jobs. Maybe not now, but once we land."

"Alright," said Gordon, "Lets print this out. Nine down, sixteen to go. What else, I say we break the list into three and pick ten each. We pitch why for each one, take the best, and then…" Again the room fell silent. The end of this exercise was a death sentence, something Gordon didn't want to say out loud.

"Yes," said the Captain, "I think that best. I'll get to it."

The room took on a deathly quiet as first only the "Vrrrrp – Vrrrrp – Vrrrrp" of the printer could be heard as it pushed out the passenger list on paper, followed by the shuffling of papers occasionally interrupted by the scratching of pens on paper. Then, as if in a human resources meeting, the candidates were presented one at a time and then four rounds of selections were made, four per group.

The first group included four data processing degrees, including a doctoral degree. The logic being they needed someone to manage, update, and create the systems with three worker bees would take care of the day to day duties and back each other up. If the ship didn't have this expertise, they might not reach New Earth, or once arrived, the new colony might very well slip back into the stone ages.

The second group included two electrical engineers, Senator Fillmore's Chief of Staff, and a Mercedes auto mechanic. The electrical engineers were selected for the same reason as the data processing, highly technical and possibly very necessary to reach New Earth. The Chief of Staff was well known for hard work, dedication to detail, and surprisingly for someone working for Senator Fillmore – a nice man. Terri always suspected that Senator Fillmore realized he needed someone who could offset the cut throat atmosphere that otherwise existed on his team. As for the Mercedes mechanic, it was claimed he could fix almost anything with a hammer, duct tape, and paper clips… and a lot more given a full set of tools. Everyone was enthusiastic about having such talent on board.

The third group included Ensign Beers and three small business men. Ensign Beers was a no brainer as the Captain's backup. As for the small businessmen, such men were needed to grow and mold communities. They were people who got things done, on time and under budget. And if they didn't, they'd try like hell to make their goals, using imagination and taking chances.

The final group was a mix. A registered nurse, the thin chef, a city planner, and Manson. The second nurse was selected since no doctors were on board. Certainly Senator Fillmore had one or more doctors available on the other rockets, but for all the obvious reasons there were no plans to wait for a health upgrade. And as Terri pointed out, younger women were needed. As to the thin chef, Terri pointed out he was thin, and would most likely take little food to eat. But none of the three mentioned the more subtle correct reasons. The thin chef was meek, weak, and timid, or so he had presented him self. Already the threads of power were working on the minds of the three headed leadership being forged. Unelected and unknown to anyone else as they decided who should live and who to die, the thin chef was no threat. They had already seen in graphic detail, the thin chef could be easily intimidated and in front of others, always a nice perk for those who are gaining in influence and power. The complete opposite of the fat chef.

The city planner was the most difficult to make the cut and was highly debated. He offered nothing of value up front. And until the colony was reached and some sort of sophisticated society was created, there would be no need for streets, subways, or any other type of infrastructure. Still, one had to look forward, if only a little. As society advanced, a lack of such knowledge could lead to sickness, inefficiency, and quite frankly an unappealing image. It was Gordon of all people who pushed for his selection. Terri gave the second needed vote, having seen in the past how her husband could make the most unusual decisions only to be proven correct later. When she saw the conviction of his belief on this matter, it was an easy vote.

The last name – Manson. Who was Manson? Nothing more than an upgrade to a janitor, or so it seemed. But Terri, with her observant eye knew what Manson really was, and this was a reason she respected Senator Fillmore. Manson, only called by his last name, was critical to the operation of the office. Not just with his always sunny personality, but his ability to keep everything in the office running. He seemed to know everyone in the Capital building and could find whatever was needed. Office supplies, podiums, drinks, food, tables... anything and everything that kept things moving. Problems might have all kinds of names, but the joke in the office was the solution was to call out one word; Manson. The three knew keeping the ship kept up and finding a way to take the disparate collection of adults selected tied properly together, no degree or resume would fix that. They needed an intangible, and that was Manson.

It was also interesting those who didn't make the cut. The bankers – all three. There was no money and therefore no need for people who would do nothing but hold other people's money. Also, all senior government officials save the Chief of Staff were denied. New Earth would be about hard work, determination, and more work. There was no use for those who marked their time dreaming of holidays, counting their sick leave accumulation, and becoming experts at making an hour of work last the entire day. Nor were any of the corporate types selected. Without any bureaucracy, there was no need for a clutch of unimaginative middle managers who were motivated by such intangibles as pensions, especially when their loyalty was most likely to the now disliked Senator Fillmore. Finally there was the huge gaggle of middle class workers Senator Fillmore saw as useful in making his life easier on board and once the space ship touched down. The committee held no grudge against these people. Successful communities have a large middle class who are the grease that keeps the gears turning. But if the gears have not yet been built, and wouldn't be for some time, what use was the middle class, especially when these were jobs anyone could learn. They were good people, the problem was good people weren't needed right now. Instead doers and the specially trained were.

The exercise of reducing over eight hundred names to twenty five had taken a little over a half hour. Still the Captain felt valuable time had been lost. And when the security warning popped onto the computer screen, showing a diagram of the ship flattened out, he wasn't surprised to see someone was once again tampering with the food bins. Grabbing a lock from a drawer, he unlocked it and placed it in his pocket. "Gordon, You know how to tag everyone we selected, do it on the screen that is? Put an 'X' next to their name?"

"Yeah – sure."

"Good. I marked the kids under fourteen. Once you update the list, sort by the 'X,' can you do that?"

"Sure, easy."

"Print that out and give it to the conductors. Everyone on the list goes to dining room B, got it? B. Including your kids. We don't need anyone suspecting."

The Captain paused to stare directly at Terri and Gordon. "If they don't get out of dining room A, there done for. Dead."

Gordon nodded and said, "B," as Terri added, "I'll go down and make sure."

"You don't need to."

"Yes I do. My kids will be down there."

"But really..."

"This is what I do, make sure things are done properly. That's how I got us on this ship. Everyone on the list is for dining room B. I got you covered."

The Captain glanced at the Johnsons a last time. Confident they were on the same page he said, "When I come back..."

"Where are you going?"

Pointing at the security warning on the screen he replied, "If my guess is right, our disobedient Admiral has snuck off the reservation again."

"And?"

Tapping the lock he said, "He isn't the only one with tricks."

"And then?"

"Meet back here... And then we'll do it."

Nothing more needed to be said, nor did anyone want to. But as the Captain again turned to leave, a voice could be heard in the room.

"Hello? Hello! Who's in there?" It was the voice of Senator Fillmore, sounding angry and in command, booming over the bridge's speakers. "Hello! Someone talk to me!"

After some quick glances the Captain made a decision. "You – Terri. Talk to him. Gordon, get the list and get our people to dining room B. I'll be back as soon as possible. Whatever you do, don't let them dock. If they do, were done for. Your whole family."

Terri decided to make a guess, saying, "And you too."

Pausing at the doorway, the Captain said, "Yes… all of us – done for."

As he disappeared, Gordon, who had finished printing the list sat down and began reviewing it.

"What the are you doing?"

"We got one chance at this, I'm going to make sure I got it right."

Terri wanted to scream, could Gordon be any more annoying? But knowing how stubborn he was, she nodded, then put a finger to his lips to make sure he was not to speak any more before saying loudly, turning up the microphone volume, "Yes. We are here."

"Is that? Is it Terri?"

Eyeing Gordon as he shuffled his papers, she said in a cold, clipped voice, "Who is this?" She could get things done when she had to, and quickly. But when delay was needed, she could play that game too.

Dinner Is Served

"Who is this? Who the hell you think it is?"

"Don't know. Please state your name." Her voice was cold and distant, unfriendly but professional.

"I need to speak to Admiral Pitts."

"Pitts?"

"Yes! Admiral Pitts! Immediately. This is Senator Fillmore."

"I'm sorry sir, Admiral Pitts has issued a new protocol."

"A new what?"

"Protocol, sir. Everyone has to be prescreened before being sent to him for approval."

Muttering under his breath Senator Fillmore said, "Damn Navy man! Can't trust anyone these days. Its gone to his head. We will see about that."

Then, his voice trembling with agitation, he asked, "Tell Admiral Pitts to come to the bridge, its Senator Larry Fillmore. Tell him to hurry. We are in rocket ship XJ1, and due to arrive for docking in…" In the background Terri could hear the Senator asking the Captain of XJ1, "How long is it?" followed by a deep voice saying, "Twenty minutes."

"Twenty minutes. I expect him to be prepared. Understand? We need to speak to him pronto."

"Well sir… first I need to find you on the passenger list. Now where did they say that was?"

"Damn it woman! Let me be blunt! I've got your Captain on board driving this ship I'm on. If you ever plan to get to New Earth… you better get your ass in gear and bring me Admiral Pitts! Got it?"

Terri was surprised that, despite disguising her voice, Senator Fillmore hadn't figured her out, from her behavior alone. After all, he'd more than once stopped to listen in awe of her stalling skills, chuckling along with the others as they listened to the conversation. But then maybe he was a little flustered. After all, decisions were now life and death, including docking to the space station. Still, she didn't expect that from Senator Fillmore, normally the coolest man in the room. Terri was rattled as well, hearing the man who could steer the space station to New Earth was on board XJ1. She still had reservations about Captain Majewski, but that would have to be dealt with later. For now she had to hold off the man who would yank her from SS 222 so that she could fall back to Earth and be broiled to death.

As Terri returned to her conversation, Gordon had collected up Jon and Mia and was headed to dining room A, clutching the list of the lucky 200. Arriving he saw the conductors waiting by the doors as if servants for the queen, rigid with hands behind their backs. Waving them over he broke the list into two parts stating, "We can't begin preparing food until everyone on this list is moved to dining room B."

The conductors sneered at Gordon, as they were trained to do. Their role on this ship was to maintain order. "And on who's direction is this? The Admiral?"

"No. Until this is done, I can't complete my structural analysis. Only after that can the Admiral assume control. We don't want that do we?" The words weren't offered as a threat or snidely. That wasn't Gordon's style. Instead it was spoken logically and without emotion.

The conductors glanced at each other, then the list. Snatching it up and splitting between them, one of the conductors said, "Very well. You may begin." As he heard the sounds of the conductors calling out names, Gordon entered dining room A as if reviewing the soundness of the floor, which also constituted the ship's hull. But he was also keeping an eye on the migration of people, and came across something he hadn't expected. The children being separated from their parents. None of this had been imagined. He wasn't prepared to see young children crying, some as little as two and three. And certainly not the parents, who stood diligently by as their children were escorted away, tears in their eyes. Still Gordon had to stay on his path. As the last children left the room, he followed behind with Jon and Mia.

"Please help me sir," said one of the conductors. He was herding the smallest children out as they screamed for their parents. Gordon stopped and looked down at the tots, and to his surprise made a snap decision, scooping the three trailing farthest behind saying to the Conductor, "Come on. Your job is to get these kids in there."

"Yes sir."

As Gordon moved to dining room B he felt disgusted in himself. As if a child molester... only worse. He was separating little children from their parents so that they could be slaughtered. When he got to the door for dining room B, depositing the children inside, he found himself staring into the eyes of Jon and Mia. Is this what a parent does? Whatever they can to save their family? Standing tall he extended an arm across the door as one of the conductors tried to enter. For some reason it felt as if the conductor entered the room, that he would be violating the agreement he made. It made no sense, but that was how it was.

"That will be all," he ordered, "You need to return, and go inside dining room A."

"Hey! You got no business telling us what to do."

"I do right now. Until this is over that is where are you supposed to be."

The conductor refused to answer, angered at being pushed around.

"Look," said Gordon in a friendlier voice, "I got my orders... from the Admiral as well."

"I thought he wasn't in charge."

"Come on. You know what he's like? I just want to do my job and get some food. We're not supposed to do it this way. You guy don't go back inside, we're all in trouble, yes?"

The conductor relaxed and after a pause said, "Ya. Ok. Make it quick."

"Sure, I'm trying. Make sure the doors are closed? All the way."

"Um, what if the Admiral returns?"

"Well then... let him in. And then close the door again."

The conductor nodded in agreement and Gordon watched as they returned to dining room A and the door closed. The Admiral. He wasn't in dining room A, so that must be who was nosing about the food bins.

As Captain Majewski arrived at the food bins, four people were surrounding food bin 001 as if on a surveillance mission. The Admiral, Captain Lipscomb, the fat chef, and the thin chef. Captain Lipscomb was tapping on the door to check its integrity.

"Sir," said Majewski with military precision.

"What the? Who the hell are you?" snarled the Admiral.

"Aw that asshole," said Lipscomb, "Wat da ya want Majewski?"

"Heard the Admiral wanted to get into the food bins."

"Yeah, so what do you want?" The tone in Lipscomb's voice was clear. He thought nothing of Majewski, a peon of sorts. And he loved treating the peons like, well peons.

The Captain glanced over at the two chefs, who were grinning at his behavior. How meek he was now that the Admiral was here.

"The codes. Are they working?"

"No," said the Admiral.

Lipscomb looked at the Admiral and understood. For now he was to be quiet while the Admiral assessed the situation.

"You got em?"

"Some of them. Yes."

"What the hell happened?"

"Don't know. Screw up in the system."

"No shit! Can you fix it?"

"Think so."

"Well then man, don't just stand there, do so."

"Ok. Over here." Majewski pushed himself to food bin 200, quickly punching in the code. Three beeps could be heard and Majewski reached for the handle. He was shoved away by Lipscomb, who snatched the door open. As it opened to reveal an empty storage container, Lipscomb said, "What the shit?"

"What?" asked the Admiral, trying to peer around the huge Lipscomb who was entering, "What the hell's the matter?" In the weightless atmosphere he was able to nudge the Captain and slip past.

Lipscomb was inside and Admiral Pitts at the door. Was it time wondered Majewski? No. There were three of them, and all were large, strong looking men. And he needed a better position.

As with the other containers, the only lighting was a dim bulb on the back wall of the bin. "See the reset button?" asked the Captain.

"I don't see a god damned thing!" replied the Admiral, now inside. "Do you Lipscomb?"

"On the wall, in the back. Made to look like one of the rivets. Push it." Placing a hand gently on the fat chef's back, Majewski shoved saying, "Go on... help."

As the fat man glided in, Lipscomb moved just outside the doorway, his military instincts taking over, protecting against a trap. Still not time thought Majewski. He could see the muscles tensing on Lipscomb. The big man needed to relax for this to work.

He leaned around Lipscomb saying, "All the way in the back. See the rivets?" Lipscomb, insulted that Majewski dared be so close to him, shoved him away, sending Majewski sailing to the other side of the aisle.

"Yeah, which one"

"Don't know. Just start pushing them. You should feel a click."

"Why the hell is this bin empty? We're supposed to have food in all of them."

"Don't know sir. I guess if in an emergency – like this – we'd need to get to the reset fast. The hidden rivet that is."

He pushed back to the door opening, subtlety pushing the thin chef to the side as he stopped, placing a hand on Lipscomb's shoulder. The huge Captain didn't flinch. That was good, he was calming down. It was almost time.

As the Admiral grumbled, "I don't see anything but goddamn rivets here, Majewski said, "Let me get something. I think this will work."

Pushing to the other wall against bin 199, he bent his legs as far as possible and launched at Lipscomb. Slamming into the big man, Majewski grabbed the handle on the door for extra leverage. If the ship had any gravity, Lipscomb would have stumbled forward and little else. But in the state of weightlessness, Lipscomb drifted erratically about as he floated into the bin, his hand scraping the doorway, sending him into an awkward spin.

Majewski continued on inside as well, the door closing behind him, turning the bulb off. Now it was a race. Who could get to the doorway first. With the Admiral, the fat chef, and Lipscomb screaming Majewski tried to remain clam, get his bearings, and move for the door. He heard more squawking as Lipscomb bumped into the Admiral and the fat chef. Reaching the door he scratched at it, trying to find the handle.

Lipscomb said, "Move, I think I got it," as Majewski ripped the door open. Clamoring outside, Majewski could see in the dim light that Lipscomb was about to launch from the back wall to the door. Slamming the door closed he fumbled about in his pocket and heard the "thump" as Lipscomb hit the door. But the big man must have missed the handle, and pulling out the lock the Captain slammed it home on the outside handle… securing the bin.

Breathing hard Majewski looked over and saw the thin chef who said meekly, "We need to let them out."

Clicking the lock secure, Majewski replied, "No, we don't."

"They will get out. We'll be in trouble."

"Don't think so." Majewski was now punching the buttons on the keypad with a constant "beep-beep-beep" and then pushed himself away. "This is one of the four extra strength meat lockers."

"And?"

"And? One… those rivets? They are there for a reason. Inch thick, maybe thicker. They're designed to be a brig if necessary. No one's breaking out of there. And two… this locker can be set for negative twenty. Don't think they will be alive very long."

"You can't do that. Why…"

Grabbing the thin man roughly Majewski said, "Why I'll tell you what. Shut up or I'll put you in another one of these. Saved your life. You should be thankful."

Looking nervously about the thin chef snipped, "Well… I don't know."

Captain Majewski didn't have time for arguing. Grabbing the thin chef by a shoulder he said, "You're coming with me."

"What… me?"

"Yes you. Don't argue. You're alive, be happy with that."

"Well… Ok, I guess. Don't kill me. Please."

"If I wanted to, you'd be in a freezer right now."

These Negotiations Are Over

Returning to the bridge the Captain expected Gordon to be there. But with only Terri in view, Captain Majewski whispered to the thin chef, "Shut up… one word and that's the end for you… got it?"

The thin chef, appearing too afraid to even offer a nod, shrank to a corner upon entering.

Terri was still in stalling mode, but running out of options. "Yes, I understand Senator Fillmore. We are trying to locate Admiral Pitts as I speak."

"The hell you are woman! I want him and now!"

Seeing he could do nothing to assist, the Captain moved to the keyboard and began typing away.

Ah, I have here… Captain Lipscomb is on his way."

"Lipscomb? Well that's better... What's that? Great! We are coming up on you. Two ships."

"What about the third?"

"Problems."

"Problems? What kind?"

"Ahhh… couldn't say exactly. Some sort of malfunction. Serious engine failure."

"Can you be more specific?"

"Um, it doesn't matter. Total loss. XJ3 will not be joining."

"What happened exactly?"

"It… aw shit, it blew the fuck up! Who cares? We are approaching on the right. Is Lipscomb there? We need someone with a brain on that bridge."

There was a subtle shake on SS 222. Not much, just the slightest tremble, as if the smallest of earthquakes. Terri glanced over at the Captain, who was smiling at the computer screen. Scrunching her face she shook her head at the Captain, who smiled in return.

"Yes, I see," said Terri, "And as for those you wanted separated from the others?"

"Yes, I see. Um, keep them at their current location. I will be reviewing their status. Print off the listing and have it available. Wow, I can't wait to get in there. What did you say your name was?"

"I didn't."

"Hmmm…" said the Senator uncomfortably, "Has Lipscomb arrived?"

"No. He apparently has gone for the Admiral."

Terri, drifted over to see what the Captain was working on. As she arrived a new screen was popping up, a schematic of the ship. The Captain typed "Layout" into the search box and a two dimension diagram for the dining rooms blinked onto the screen. Clicking on "File" a dropdown menu appeared including a line stating, "Dining Rooms" Moving the mouse over the words, a sidebar menu appeared with the letters A, B, C, and D. The Captain clicked on A and the diagram zoomed in to show dining room A. Again the Captain clicked "File" and then "Doors." A popup menu showed "Lock" and "Unlock." But both words were grayed out... somewhere a door to dining room A was open.

"I got to go," said the Captain, "Keep an eye on him." Pushing away from the computer and floating to the door, the Captain pointed at the thin chef threatening, "Nothing. Say nothing."

"Say," said the Senator, "You know... you got a slight rotation to the ship. You know that? Nobody hit the thrusters did they?"

"Senator?"

"You've got a spin, understand me? Your spinning. We can't dock like that. You've got to lose the spin. No... what's that Captain? The Captain here just told me you've got to reverse the thruster engine. It shouldn't take much to stop the spin. Why... it's barely visible, didn't see that before. If we try docking, were so big it might rip the docking mechanism to bits. Got to be exact."

"Spin? I don't feel any."

"We are almost along side you now. Yes, you are spinning. If you can't get the spin out. Big problems. What? Oh, it seems the Admiral won't be of use on this. We need, what's his title? Oh, I don't remember."

"Majewski?"

"Maybe. I can't remember. Get Admiral Pitts, or Lipscomb. Lipscomb is better."

"So Lipscomb can do this?"

"No. But he'll know who can."

Suddenly the thin chef screamed, "Senator! Admiral Pitts has been kidnapped, as has Lipscomb. These people… they've hijacked this ship! They threw the Admiral and Lipscomb in a freezer and are killing them. They turned the temperature all the way down. They'll be dead in a few hours… or less. You've got to get on board, and hurry!"

"Shut up!" snapped Terri as she charged the thin chef. But she quickly found that while for a man, the thin chef was small and frail, compared to a woman he was slightly oversized. As they wrestled about, the Senator asked, "What? What was that?"

"They've seized the ship! The structural engineer and his wife… and one of your men. They just did something to make the ship spin. Hurry up or we're all lost. You, me, everyone."

"Well then man, get to… get to… the others. Yes, get help. We can win this fight!"

The thin chef began pounding on Terri's arms, loosening her grip. Then as she slipped below his waist, he began to knee her as they cartwheeled about the cabin. He escaped a first time, and was caught, again he escaped, pushing his way to the door before being grabbed again. With his arms free, he began to pull himself out of the bridge toward dining room A. The going was slow but Terri's was slipping. It seems the thin chef was in great shape and stronger than he looked.

Finally, he broke free and began to dart away. Terri wanted to shout, but who would she alert? And where the hell was Gordon? Fortunately it didn't occur to the thin chef to shout. They were halfway to the dining room when the Captain came into view, saying, "What the?"

"He's going to dining room A… Are the doors closed?"

"Um, yes."

"Then get them locked! Both rooms, A and B! I'll find Gordon."

It was a race now. Could the thin chef beat the Captain? The thin chef was quick, darting about like a minnow, pushing himself along. But the battle with Terri was finally sapping his energy as the Captain, now understanding the situation, was pulling forward as if his life depended on it.

As he slipped into the bridge the Captain could hear the Senator screaming, "We've got to get on board. Damn it Captain, get us in there."

Another the voice on rocket XJ1 replied as the Captain reached the computer, "We can't just dock, there's another rocket attached to the space station, if we mess up, it's spinning around and smash into us, I've only got so much fuel left… fumes really."

The Captain clicked on the screen with his mouse. The screen blinked and then the words "Locked – Dining Room A" appeared. "Whoo-hoo!"

"What? Who the hell was that? Terri? Is that you? Damn you! After all we did for you?"

"You mean the list?" shouted Captain Majewski, "The list to be returned to earth? That kind of help?"

"What are you talking about?"

"We know about what is going on down there. We know XJ3 was blasted to bits. We know temperatures are in the two hundred range. That list. The list of those scheduled to die."

There was no response from the Senator.

"Yes, that's right, *Senator*. And you are right. There are some people who will die. But let me inform you now. These negotiations… are over."

Who Shall Fly This Ship For Me?

The sounds of a distant banging were echoing up to the bridge. On the computer screen was the schematic for dining room B and the popup menu for locking the doors visible, the mouse hovering over the word "Lock." Where was Gordon wondered the Captain. It was a simple decision, put everyone on lockdown – get control of the ship – and sort it out from there. But the word "Lock" stubbornly remained grayed out, meaning it was inaccessible. Finally... in the blink of an eye the word transformed to a solid, deep black font and with a click on the word the words "Locked – Dining Room B" appeared on the screen.   But who was in the dining room, and more importantly, who was out. If the thin chef had somehow managed to get to dining room B... had alerted them. A mob could be coming to stop their mutiny... and that could mean in the long run he was dead.

The sounds of someone – or several people – approaching were easy to hear. What could he do but wait? There wasn't anywhere to hide, not for long. Glancing around the bridge, the Captain minimized the screen and locked the computer. No one was going to do anything without his approval. As to waiting for his fate? No, he would fight. Three men entered the bridge – all looking determined, angry, and ready for action. The Captain with one strong push launched himself out of the bridge. As the men called after him to return, the Captain disappeared down the hallway.

The men who entered gave the appearance of being determined, but were hardly what could be considered muscular or fit. In fact one of them was already sweaty from the exercise and breathing heavily. "Who was that?" he asked between heaves.

"Don't know," said the second, "Saw him briefly when we first came on board. Something to do with the staff to fly this ship, that is if his clothing means anything."

The first man nodded and said, "I suppose you're right."

"Who is that? You sound familiar. This is Senator Fillmore."

The out of shape man looked around for the source of the voice saying, "Senator?"

"Yes!"

"Senator, This is Jim LaBlanc."

"LaBlanc? Hallelujah!" Then the Senator's tone changed, as if barking orders to a subordinate.

"LaBlanc! Get me on board... now!"

"Yes sir," said LaBlanc dutifully, "Just as soon as we get things settled down in here."

"Damn it no! I need to be on board LaBlanc. Do your job and make it happen! Don't fuck with me!" The Senator was a master of negotiations and knew, only the inner circle had any power. As for all others, no matter what they were told, they could only wait to discover what they were to get... or rather be allowed. And that meant it would be what was left after the inner circle took what they wanted. Senator Fillmore wanted to be in that inner circle.

But there was a surprising amount of steel in LaBlanc's response. "No sir. We are waiting."

"Waiting? For what?"

"Waiting for the situation here to be secured."

"Get Admiral Pitts! He can do the securing. You get on your job and secure my ass on that ship! He might be locked away."

Turning to the third man LaBlanc said calmly, "How do we put him on mute?"

"Um, sure... I'll do it right now."

After a short amount of searching the mute button was pushed. "Ok. Want the sound off as well?"

"No. I want to hear what he is saying. In fact, can you turn it up? I heard voices in the background." LaBlanc's voice was professional, businesslike, and assured. As if he was in charge, not the Senator, nor the others with him. LaBlanc was in his bearing, tone, and even haircut – dull and conservative – a Washington insider. A man who had carved out his own world and was comfortable in it.

"Sure, that's easy. What now?"

"Now? We wait."

"For?"

LaBlanc glanced up as if that was an annoying question. "I wish I knew. That means we need to play this out." The tone in LaBlanc voice meant the conversation was over.

But if LaBlanc was quiet, the same couldn't be said for Senator Fillmore who kept up a regular banter, which was mostly ignored until he said, "LaBlanc! LaBlanc! Did they tell you about landing? Once we get to new earth, you need the rockets. Ask your Captain Majewski. Tell them."

LaBlanc considered the words before saying, "What's the Senator talking about?"

The man working the computer said, "Yeah. My understanding is that we'll use the nuclear power on board to travel there, but once we arrive at new earth, we'll have to land. The way it works is as we fall through the atmosphere, the rockets fire their thrusters to slow the descent. Then, when we get close, they pop parachutes and push out wings to glide us in for a soft landing.

"No shit. I thought the rockets were only for taking people to the space crafts. I guess it wouldn't look too good if the people on earth knew the rockets weren't coming back."

"Yup. Once everything is in place, its easy really. Most of it done by computer. But you need someone to man the computer. Like that guy who jumped out of here."

"Anyone else?"

"Yeah. The Captain of the Rocket the Senator is on. I think one other, he's already on board. Oh and then there is Lipscomb, or he claims he can. Don't think he always manages to do what he says."

"Hmmm. Was he in our dining room?"

"Um, yeah, I guess so."

"So what the hell is going on?"

"Excuse me?"

"We are removed from the main dining room... with the children. Then screaming and yelling from the main dining room, but the door is locked. Inside they're screaming bloody murder of a mutiny. This Gordon Johnson fellow gets all nervous and grabs Manson to show him something. What he won't say. Tells us to head to the bridge to talk to the Captain, and when we arrive, he takes off."

"That's the size of it."

The two men were interrupted by the Senator, who barked, "Jim, get me on now. We're short of fuel. And what's that? Hang on a second. Maybe air too. One of these rockets didn't get extra oxygen on it. You've got to stop the spin on the ship. We can't dock until you stop that. Damn it Jim, you're my Chief of Staff. I pay you to get things done."

Turning the mute button off Jim said, "Spin? How do we do that?"

"Hell I don't know. There's a main computer. Get on there. That's your main priority. I need to be on that bridge pronto!"

Turning the mute back on Jim asked the man at the computer, "Got it?"

"Naw. It's locked. Can't do anything without the password."

Jim frowned, his lips little more than a line as he said, "Well. Maybe that's best for now. Until I find out what all this craziness is about."

"How's that?"

"How long you work for the Senator?"

"Oh, my wife just started, I'm a contractor."

"I've known him for twenty years. You don't want him around when things get thin."

"Thin? What do you mean?"

"I don't know. But I'll find out. That's what I do."

"Yes sir. And from what I hear, you're the best at it. And as for the Senator? What are we to do?"

"Well. That's a tricky one. He's really not a Senator anymore if you know what I mean."

"How's that?"

Well, he's a Senator from the great State of Arkansas."

"Yeah."

"From what we are hearing, there's no Arkansas anymore. Nor any United States, or anything else for that matter."

"So?"

"So he's not a Senator anymore. We're on our own up here. From the reports I got, the whole thing is going to melt down in the next twenty four hours. He's just another man, unelected by anyone up here."

"Well, I guess so. You thinking of taking over yourself?"

Jim LaBlanc looked over at Kevin, a man he didn't know too well. But then Kevin obviously didn't know him much either. He wasn't a man who coalesced and consolidated power for his own use. No, Jim was content to stay in the shadows and work quietly toward his goals, arm twisting, cajoling, and persuading.

"That ain't my style. The Senator is the type who leads. But before we get him on board, let's get things straight. It'll just be more trouble otherwise when he arrives."

"What? What are you talking about?"

Jim said nothing, but as if on queue Senator Fillmore snarled, "Jim. What the hell is the problem? I'm beginning to lose my temper here, and you know what that means."

Hiding In Plain Sight

If one is going to hide, where to go? That was the problem facing Captain Majewski. The ship was huge, no doubt of that. But as the ship was hollow and laid out in a fairly uniform format, SS 222 did not possess a variety of nooks and crannies perfect for concealment. As of now the plan was falling apart. He had no idea where Gordon or Terri were, and the bridge had been surrendered to those he assumed were supporters of Senator Fillmore. He didn't want to die, but circumstances were beginning to point that. He could be thrown off the ship for the murder of Admiral Pitts, Lipscomb, and the fat chef if nothing else. But really what other options were there? He already was on the list marked for death. As he moved about the ship trying to find a hideaway, he began to realize such thinking would get him nowhere. He needed a solution, not complaints.

So what were the positives? It took awhile, but finally it occurred to him, the Senator's personal pit bull, Admiral Pitts and his right hand man Captain Lipscomb were locked away. If it came to a physical battle, those would be the two most aggressive opponents. As for the fat chef, he might be a kind father and loving husband, but right now? Captain Majewski was happy the obnoxious fat man was locked away.

And then more good news came to him. Originally five people had the ability to unlock the main computer; Lipscomb, one of the other ensigns, the Captain of the rocket ship holding the Senator, the Senator, and himself. But that didn't matter because Captain Majewski had changed the password. If he died, then so too would everyone else. Not a nice way to consider things, but the truth. And sometimes one had to make decisions for survival, and this was the kind of leverage that would keep him alive and protect him – even from Gordon and Terri.

He was feeling better but that still didn't address the problem – where to hide. As he approached the food bins... was that Gordon? Moving closer he heard a voice, but not Gordon. Someone was banging about, but the scratchy voice was anything but Gordon's. He could take refuge in one of the food bins, but what good would that do? Trapped in a small cell with only one way out, might as well consider that sending himself to jail.

After glancing about he slid over to bin 200 and rapped on the door. A weak tap responded. They were still alive. Maybe he could let them go, say it was a misunderstanding. No, another foolish idea. First Pitts and Lipscomb would lock him up, and they wouldn't show mercy to him. And this would bring the Senator on board, who would promptly ship him back to Earth and death. As he thought about this act of kindness, he realized there wasn't a better place on the ship for the obnoxious Admiral Pitts and his brutish lackey Lipscomb.

Without further consideration of their plight, Caption Majewski moved on, pushing back and forth through the hallway finding a litany of empty rooms, sniffing about like a hungry fox hunting mice or other small prey. But to no avail, there was nothing on the ship other than bent steel. It was as if he was inside a huge empty can of soda.

More noises could be heard, this time in front. He paused, after all, who else had escaped from dining room B? But as the sounds were rather faint, he decided to chance a look and gliding up to peer around the corner he saw to his relief Terri, who was moving about as if searching for something.

"Terri," he hissed quietly.

She started at the comment, and realizing it was the Captain, said in a rather friendly tone, "Oh, there you are."

"What are you doing?"

"Looking for Gordon. Didn't want to go to the dining areas in case the chef got to the door and opened it before you could lock it."

"I did, or I think so. I'm looking for Gordon as well. Well not really. It'd be nice to know where he is, but it's more important to get control of this ship again."

"Control? What do you mean?"

Biting a lip at his failure, the Captain said, "The bridge. They got control."

"Who? Who has control?"

"Don't know. When they rushed in, I left."

"What did they look like? Where'd they come from?"

"Don't know that either. Could be anyone. I just knew leaving was my only option."

"Anyone? No. We need to know. Can they communicate with the rocket the Senator is on? Did you turn the mike off?"

"Um, no…" said the Captain guiltily. He'd been so busy with locking down the computer he didn't think of the microphone, which had a rare momentarily silent Senator on line.

"Oh god. We've got to… oh I don't know. We need to know who they are! If they let the Senator on. He'll kill us. Me… Gordon… the kids."

At first the Captain didn't know what to say, but trying to be positive he said, "We've still got control."

"How is that?" she snapped angrily, "We're here and they are on the bridge."

"I locked it down. The main computer. No one is going anywhere without my say so."

"That so?"

"Yeah. And no one is locking onto this ship as long as we are spinning."

"Spinning?"

"Yeah. Didn't you feel the shake? That was the maneuvering jets, not a lot… enough to get us spinning. As big as these ships are, they'll tear each other to pieces if they try to dock."

Terri took a moment to take in the Captain's comments. It didn't sound so good. The idea of the ships ripping apart. "So where's Gordon?"

"To be honest, I don't know. But I know where we should go."

"Where?"

"The dining rooms. I locked them down. Both of them. Let's see if anyone is outside. And maybe figure out who's inside."

"Then what?"

"I guess find a good hiding place until we figure out how to move forward."

Slipping past the food bins the voices could be heard again, but when Terri paused to try to figure out who, the Captain grabbed her by the arm saying, "Come on. One thing at a time."

Arriving at the dining rooms they found nothing but sealed doors. Grabbing the handle to one the doors Captain gently tried to open it. It didn't budge.

"Can they break through?" whispered Terri.

"No. The rooms are designed so that if a hole punctures the outside, the seal will hold. Walls, ceilings, doors, everything."

Frowning, Terri said, "A coffin."

Glancing at Terri, the Captain said, "Yup, a coffin. But not ours, not yet. Let's check the other one."

As Terri jiggled the door a voice from within could be faintly heard saying, "Who's that?"

"Don't worry, we are getting ready to let you out."

"What about the mutiny? The chef told us. Didn't you?"

Another voice could be heard saying, "Yes. I told you."

The Captain smiled. The thin chef had actually won their race. But made the mistake of entering room A, allowing the door to close. Maybe, very likely in fact, the occupants of dining room B had no idea of what was going on. He couldn't say why, but he felt good about that. Smiling he said, "Ok. Now it would be nice to know who has taken over the bridge."

"You say the computer is locked down?"

"Yup. Completely."

"Ok, let me ask this, is there a communicator on the computer, the kind where you can type messages back and forth between computers."

"Sure, but there aren't any other computers on board."

"If there was, can you send them messages, and get them back? Without losing control of the computer?"

"Um, yeah, think so, but you told me. Nothing. No other computers."

Again Terri became silent. Then she said, "Come on. The engine rooms."

"The what? Why?"

"Supposed to have a backup computer. That is if they put it in. Whoever stocked this space lab was smart enough to put in just enough to pass inspection. And that should have meant the backup computer station, in the engine room."

"And why would they put that in?"

"In order to test the engines, you have to communicate with the bridge, and that would be done through the computers. Plus that computer monitors the engine activity. That would be checked out for sure in any pre-check. Hopefully that is."

"Great, if that's true."

"You've got any better ideas?"

"Nope. Let's get going."

"I wonder where Gordon is."

"He's fine. After all, he couldn't leave the ship, could he?"

"No, I guess not."

Watching Them Die Like Ants

Jim LaBlanc was in the process of calming Senator Fillmore down, something he was an old hand at. One didn't have to work long with the Senator to realize this was often needed, sometimes a constant problem that was tougher to remove than an iron stain in a bathroom tub. With the computer locked down there was no way to stop the space station from spinning, and none of the Senator's alternate solutions were viable. Not the, 'Send someone to get me,' nor the, 'Just reboot the damn thing,' and definitely not, 'Tie a rope to us and pull us over.' The last seemed a carryover from an untold number of campaign speeches where the Senator always felt obligated to offer a solution that was homespun and simplistic. The Senator claimed such comments were offered to make sure he connected with everyone in the room, no matter how stupid they were.

As the Senator tried to continue this pointless conversation, the computer screen in the bridge blinked on.

Saying, "Senator, hang on a moment. We got something here," Jim scrambled over to the screen." After much blinking and some clicks, the main screen came up and almost immediately disappeared.

Then the words, <<Can we talk?>> appeared on the screen.

Jim glanced at Kevin and then the third man before typing in, <<Sure>>, punching the "Enter" button with authority.

There was a pause, then, <<Who are we speaking to?>>

Jim was an expert at such banter, replying quickly with, <<You first.>>

Finally an answer came. <<Captain Majewski.>>

"Captain Majewski? Kevin, you know of anyone like that? Check the register."

"Can't. It's only on the computer. I know a lieutenant Majewski."

Nodding LaBlanc typed in, <<You mean Lieutenant Majewski?>>

<<No>>

<<I'm not aware of any Captain Majewski. Please explain.>>

<<Sure. You may not know me as that right now. But you will, once we talk. Who am I talking to?>>

Jim didn't want to answer. He wanted to be in control of this conversation. They needed to provide answers to him. He was Chief of Staff for Senator Fillmore and had been for some time. Experience had taught him you didn't find out anything – at least of value – letting others meander around the facts. So instead he typed, <<You haven't answered my question.>> And then he waited… and waited. It was called the pregnant pause. It rattled ninety nine percent of all people and would work here. And so he waited, and waited, and waited. Finally there was a response.

<<Who are you?>>

Not what he wanted. Frowning he typed once more, <<Answer my question.>>

<<I'll not die>> was the cryptic answer.

<<Why would I want you dead?>>

<<If you don't know, then maybe I'm not talking to the right person.>>

Jim recognized the insult immediately. <<Then why contact me?>>

<<Didn't mean to. Please put me in contact with someone in charge.>>

Seeing the message Kevin asked, "Maybe he means the Senator?"

As the Senator, hearing his title said, "What… what's that? You need me?"

Jim frowned at Kevin and pushed the mute button on the Senator's feed before saying, "No Kevin. We are fine right here."

"Yeah but…"

"Look. Let me do my job. Don't worry about this."

"Ok, but I think he means…"

"Shhhh! I'll handle this."

Jim turned off the mute and returned to the screen typing, <<You've got the right person. Answer my question.>>

<<How's this for an answer. People are going to die. Do you want to be on that list?>>

<<So you are a terrorist?>>

<<No. A realist. I suggest you be the same. It'll be better for all of us in the long run. To start, who am I talking with? I gave you my name. Don't like my title, so be it. I'll give no more information until I get a name.>>

Jim rubbed his chin. These things take time. He'd get his information. He always did. This Captain Majewski or whoever it was could be difficult or not. Jim was an old hand at these things, not the type to get flustered at the first snide comment. And so he was happy when Senator Fillmore interrupted with the announcement, "Hey! Jim! The other rocket has arrived! Remember, I'm to board first. Got it?"

Jim typed, <<Got to go. Other urgent matters need my attention.>>

"It looks like he's coming in hot," stated the Senator with excitement, "Might be running out of oxygen."

LaBlanc shoved over to the bridge's side windows and could see the rocket ship approaching quickly, every so often firing its maneuvering jets to slow the rocket down. "Kevin, can you get us to the docking area?"

"Sure."

"Then let's go, and hurry it up."

As the Senator continued to scream about being the next on the ship, Jim and Kevin pushed, jumped, and pulled their way to the docking area. Arriving they could see the nose of the new rocket slowly pulling past the docking area as the ship rolled too far to properly engage. With a last blast of it's rockets, the ship stopped beside the space station as the docking door continued to roll out of position. Then there was the sound of steel grating on steel, as if pushed heavily against resistance. Then the door to the rocket opened and one of the rocket's crew leapt out of the ship and landed on the surface of the space station, only inches from Jim, mouth wide open, eyes bugged out, either dead or in the process of dying.

And then, like fire ants rushing out to defend their lair, out came the rest of the passengers. Crew members, men, women, and children, one clutching a handful of jewel necklaces. And all with the same open expression that spoke of desperation and a lack of oxygen. As one pointed at the hatch door, Jim looked down at the round handle. He could turn it and try to let them in, save them.

But even as he reflexively moved a hand to do so, Kevin grabbed it saying, "No. You'll kill all of us."

Jim looked at Kevin, and could see the look of shock on his face. He was right. You don't open a hatch in outer space. Glancing one more time at the frozen faces, one banging lightly on the wall to the space station, Jim couldn't take it anymore.

He shoved away from the hull, spinning away from the close up horror of death in outer space. He couldn't deal with that. He was a strong man. Not physically, but mentally, emotionally, and lots of other ways. But he wasn't prepared for this. He had come down hoping to possibly save five hundred people. Instead he had watched them die in some sort of odd way, as if in an outer body experience, the face of the first crew member who came so close to him burned into his memory.

Soon he was joined by Kevin who gently put a hand on his shoulder. Somehow it didn't help. It seemed so out of form, using a personal touch for the death of so many in the vast void of emptiness of space. And that was how he felt. They were the last of their kind. Blasting off to take advantage of technology no one believed in. Heading to a planet that had a good chance of being a huge fireball, or so he was told. And that was one of the good prospects. It was all… empty now. Space, earth, this ship. They didn't belong here. But what could he do? As they slowly returned to the bridge, Jim's breath was shallow and his forehead sweaty. He didn't want this, not right now.

Entering the bridge, there was a question on the screen. <<Who are you?>> Right now he didn't really know. Some sort of air breathing animal. Nothing more than a brain with a bunch of attachments such as a liver and feet that allowed him to move about and survive. But that wouldn't mean much as a response.

Feeling an overwhelming numbness he typed <<Jim LaBlanc>> and paused. Finally he punched the enter key and the message was sent. What else could he do? Ultimately, what did it matter?

Of Treachery, Treason, and Skullduggery

<<Jim? This is Terri Johnson.>>

Jim stared at the screen. It took some time for the words to register. Terri. Terri Johnson. Sure he knew her. Worked with him at Senator Fillmore's office on Capital Hill. They had always been friends, kindred spirits if you will. Both cheerful in their work, respectful, and hard working. The kind of person he liked working with. As those memories passed through his mind, he started to return to his old self, and began typing.

      <<Terri? Why all the mystery?>>

      <<Wasn't me. We've got a situation.>>

      <<Don't I know it.>>

      <<You have no idea.>>

      <<Really? You didn't see what I just did.>>

      <<What's that?>>

      <<Never mind. What do you got?>>

      <<A problem.>>

      <<And that is?>>

      <<Senator Fillmore.>>

      <<The Senator? How's that?>>

      <<Do you know about the list?>>

      <<Which one. We've got lots.>>

      <<The listing of those to be returned to Earth.>>

Jim paused. He wasn't aware of any such list. But it really didn't surprise him. The Senator was cut throat, always had been. Would do anything to get ahead. In this business you had to be. But a list of those to be sent back to Earth? Why? The answer hit him as soon as he asked it. The last rockets to take off were overloaded, or so Senator Fillmore had stated to him a short while ago. And the Senator wasn't one to live life on the edge… of comfort that is. If it meant sending some people back to die, he wouldn't have a problem with that. After all, the remaining three rockets were half full, all because the Senator wanted to have personal belongings. In fact everyone on the first rocket ship was only allowed a knapsack of clothing, no real technology, or other valuables. Even the amount of jewelry worn was limited. The explanation was weight, but Jim knew better.

The Senator was controlling, always had been. But with the advent of recent events, he seemed to take it to a higher level. It was to the point Jim was a little nervous about the Senator's behavior, and what he might become when they landed on this foreign planet… away from law, order, democracy, and civilization. Jim had always found it interesting how kings became tyrants. It was no different today. Men and power – the more they had, the more it was abused. How many political junkets had he made to obscure countries and met with men who had killed their enemies, own people, members of their families, as if cattle to be slaughtered? And all for power. He couldn't say. Would Senator Fillmore be the same? Or would he be above the fray, a benevolent dictator. Dictator, and not elected leader, Jim had already seen that in the Senator. The closer they came to lift off, the more he spoke of himself and his duty. Duty as leader that is. Never any mention of elections or freedom.

And then there was Admiral Pitts and Captain Lipscomb. Jim LaBlanc had great respect for the military. But he'd also had the displeasure of a few dinners when these two military men were in attendance. Their stories, always told with a grin and a laugh spoke of behavior that to say the least was less than a gentleman. What would they become if given free rein to behave as they wished? He tried not to think of such things, it was because of Senator Fillmore that he was on this space station. One had to make deals in Washington, that was the way it was. This was one of the ugliest he'd ever had agreed to, but when your family is in danger, you do what you have to. What was the other option? Stay on Earth?

As to personal belongings, he may have been limited as all the others in the weight limit and content. But Jim had more belongings, tucked away in one of the three remaining rockets, as did the Admiral and Captain Lipscomb. He was, as long as he stayed in the good favor of Senator Fillmore, part of the upper caste of society... barely. Not like the rest on the first rocket. They were indentured servants, who would toil away so that the Senator and his friends could live a life of ease. And that was where people like Terri came in.

<<What about this list?>>

<<Sent just before lift off.>>

<<And?>>

<<And? And my husband, me, and our children are on that list.>>

<<Well,>> typed Jim, frowning grimly at Kevin, <<I don't think we have that problem anymore.>>

<<I do.>>

<<Like I said, you don't know what I know.>>

<<Neither do you. What do you got?>>

It was an odd comment. Terri was a great girl and a wonderful employee. But there was always an unseen line. Jim was Chief of Staff and she was just one of the others. He expected and always was treated with respect by her. But this? It was a request, as if… not equals, but she was the superior. It irked him slightly.

<<No, you go first.>>

<<Where's Gordon?>>

Again, Terri was always so obedient. Now suddenly she was being brusk and aggressive.

<<Went with Manson, wanted to show him something. Don't know what.>>

<<I know. What you got?>>

He didn't want to answer. But maybe this would put her into place. <<I just saw XJ3 pull into dock. Everyone dead. That should settle your worries.>>

<<Nope. Not in the least. We got bigger problems.>>

<<Bigger? Bigger than watching five hundred people die? Don't think so.>>

<<Yes. Much.>>

Jim stared at the screen. It had been the most horrific scene he'd ever witnessed, just a few short minutes ago. And here Terri, an office girl, was telling him that was nothing? What could possibly trump that? But something was warning Jim. Terri was a clever girl, not one to boast and brag. Raising his hands he slowly pushed the sides of his hair back, trying to think what could be worse than what he'd just seen.

Typing slowly as he chose his words he clacked out, <<Ok… What's bigger?>>

There was a pause and then came, <<This is Captain Majewski. How about your family dying?>>

Yup. That was bigger. And further, Jim LaBlanc didn't take kindly to threats. Instantly angered, he typed, <<What's that mean?>>

<<Exactly what it meant. You've no idea what were dealing with here. Not a clue. I told you I'm Captain Majewski. You better start to change your view of things. Everyone's life is on the table now, including mine. I plan on making it through to the end, how about you? Does that get your attention?>>

<<Yes, you already had it.>>

<<No I didn't. You wanted to play games. You've no idea. I'm going to survive, and if you want to as well, then I suggest you realize what you're up against.>>

<<Ok, tell me. What am I up against?>>

Again there was a pause, and then, <<This is Terri again. Where is Gordon? Are you supposed to meet up with him?>>

Gordon? What did her husband have to do with all this?

<<Don't know.>>

<<Find him. Talk to him. You won't believe what he's going to tell you. I'm guessing that's why he brought Manson with him. Everyone trusts him. We can't go any further until then. Let us know when you find Gordon and Manson and talk to them. Then you'll understand what we are about.>>

Why couldn't they just tell him? They threaten his family, and then... this? <<That's all you can tell me?>>

<<How about this. This is Captain Majewski. Pitts, Lipscomb, and some fat chef. They are dead. I killed them. I'm not playing. I don't want to hurt you, but we've already decided all this. I'm not throwing names on the table again. Talk to Gordon, and then contact us.>>

Jim scratched an ear, pondered the words, and then looked over at Kevin before shrugging his shoulders. Kevin stared at the words on the screen, and shrugged his shoulders in answer. It didn't make any sense. Tapping the screen, Kevin said, "Want to go find this Gordon fellow?"

"Sure," said Jim, "What else can we do at this point?"

Pushing the Mute button Kevin said, "Should we tell the Senator?"

"No. Five hundred dead? And they say they got something worse. What's worse than that? This girl Terri. She's a straight shooter. If she says she's got something, well then darn it, she does. Or so I'm guessing. Gordon is her husband. Met him a few times. Bit of a tight ass, but he can be trusted. As much as one can."

"Anything else?"

"Yeah, we'll use Manson. Like Terri said, he's never steered me wrong. I don't know enough to trust Gordon, but Manson, he's pulled us out of some fires. Nothing big, but if he says something, you can bank on it. And I know how to read him."

"So what do you think it is?"

"Bigger than watching five hundred die before your eyes? You got me. That's for sure. Almost don't want to know."

I Want What I Want!

Senator Fillmore was at his wits end. Close to exhausting the remainder of his fuel there were no proper docking procedures if the space station was spinning. Not safely that is. But that wasn't the worse of it, not as far as the Senator was concerned. Something was going on, and to find out, he needed to be on the space station. Never had Jim LaBlanc been so evasive. Not that he was overly so. It seemed lately he'd put some distance between him and the Senator. Nothing much, but the Senator noticed everything. But then Jim had known the Senator forever. Sure it might be an insult having gone on the first rocket – with the peasants if you will – but Jim wasn't one of them. The upper class that is. Always plain and boring. One wife, never cheated. Talked about his kids, didn't drink, not like the Senator. Went home at night.

And the Senator, well… he was a legend, at least in his opinion. His life had been a litany of booze, women, and power, the way he liked it. While others worried and cried about the destruction of the Earth, secretly he was eager for it. He was going to his own planet. Everything would have to be redone or created. No sub-committees, late night votes, or other annoyances of democracy. Finally the power to run things as he saw fit. And with people who would get things done his way. Admiral Pitts for one. That's the kind of man he wanted. A doer, not someone who sat on the sidelines like… well like LaBlanc. Maybe that was the problem. LaBlanc had always been a necessity. Someone to make nice with others. But now they were going where nice wasn't necessary. His own planet, where he could make his own rules. What could be finer? Possibly LaBlanc was beginning to realize he was soon to become a relic, a worthless bureaucrat that no longer served any significant purpose. Reduced to a message boy and little more.

First he had to get on that damn space station. How difficult could it be? Stop the spinning, and dock. That was it. They were in place, the space station wasn't. Despite his frustration, he remained calm, until the body floated by that is. Had to be from XJ3. Something obviously had gone wrong, very wrong. Maybe they were out of air. These rockets were prepped in a rush, or air held back as a bargaining chip, and one might not have been given its full measure... that was the concern anyway. Whatever. When the body floated past, eyes and mouth wide open, that was a call to action. If they wouldn't let him on, then damn it, he'd get on there himself... somehow. That's the way he was. He wanted what he wanted, and when he wanted it. That's all there was to it. He didn't wait or compromise. Not anymore. Not right now at least in the middle of space with limited supplies.

And where the hell were Pitts and Lipscomb? He signed them on because they were certifiable fire eaters, and they couldn't seem to find their way to the bridge. Incompetent clowns! This was specifically what he wanted them for, put them on the first rocket specifically for this. Get control! And they were the types to do it. Break regulation, and in a heartbeat. Hell, who cared what the rules were anymore? Earth was melting down. As far as he could tell, SS 222 was Earth. The last of the earthlings. Them and a few other lucky ships... maybe. He knew darn well most of the planets found were completely uninhabitable. In fact, it was a huge gamble the planet they were headed for was survivable. As for the Captain of this rocket ship, he offered nothing in the way of solutions, whining over and over again the same crap about safety and procedure. Where did they find these guys? Again, he was supposed to be able to handle any situation, or so it was said. Instead this Captain only offered complaints and warnings.

But finally they caught a break. The space station shook violently, but more importantly, the spin slowed considerably. The Senator didn't care why, what he knew was a window of opportunity was now slowly turning toward him when the space station docking bay would return into view.

Away from his line of sight the reason for the reduction in spin was easy to see. XJ3, now a skeleton ship void of any crew, had bumped into XJ4, attached to the hull of SS 222. Had it only been attached by the hatch, disaster would have ensued. But XJ4 had been fully locked down for its travel to New Earth, so instead of breaking up the space station, XJ3 somehow clawed onto XJ4, with XJ3 was now wedged between XJ4 and the space station. As a result and as Senator Fillmore noted, the space station's rotation was much slower. Not perfect for docking, but possibly slow enough to make an attempt... maybe.

They had just missed the docking station, but it would come around again. In the meantime Captain Boz – what a silly name – needed to bring the ship into position.

"Captain. Captain! Did you see that? Something happened."

"Yeah, I saw it."

"Get in position. We can dock, soon as it comes around again!"

But Boz, in typical fashion said, "Now hold on, we don't know what caused that. Aught to find out what's going on first."

The Senator had enough of his excuses. Now was the time to strike. "Damn it you coward! When that dock comes round again, you better be in position!"

"Take it easy. I served three tours, saw combat in each."

"Then what the hell's wrong with you? Go!"

"We've only got so much fuel. It's a miracle I got us here, considering we were practically on the wrong side of the planet when launched."

In a snide, almost childish voice Senator Fillmore repeated, "Practically on the wrong side." Then in his normal, angry voice, he continued, "If I listened to people like you, I couldn't get elected chief moron to No Shit, Kansas. Get our ass over there and now."

Boz hesitated. He knew enough from the many junkets he had captained back and forth from Earth. It was much more unforgiving up here. The slightest mistake got people killed. But the Senator didn't want to hear that. Boz knew that once on board, he was to be the main officer in charge of daily activities regarding flying SS 222. Further he knew that once on New Earth... he was worthless. Once the space station landed, that might be it for manned flight for some time. What good was a lifelong pilot in a society of the horse and buggy... or close to it. Not much. But the Senator? The way things were going, he was going to be... what? Supreme leader? Whatever it was, you didn't want to be on his wrong side once they arrived. If you were on his good side? The Senator treated those he liked very well thank you.

It wasn't as if Boz wasn't opposed to standing up to authority. Had done it many times. If it wasn't for the fact he might very well be the best pilot of his generation, Captain Boz could have been prisoner Boz, or dishonorably discharged Boz, or just a drunk... a drugged up has been. Been all of those briefly. But he wasn't, not right now. His flying skills pulling him out of innumerable scraps, brawls, and disasters. He was so good he had earned a chance to fly SS 222 to a new planet and life. Something about entering the seventh dimension being rather tricky. Whatever the reason, he was here, and had a chance to survive the destruction of Earth.

So after expressing a sour grimace at the Senator's command, he carefully began to use the auxiliary jets to maneuver the rocket into docking position. It was a slow process with the conflicting forces of no gravity allowing the slightest push to have an effect and the huge mass of the rocket which occasionally required an extra blast of energy. Flying a rocket ship. He considered it similar to dancing with a fat woman. Sometimes you didn't have to do a thing, being pulled along wherever she wanted to go. And other times... look out. Crashing about and out of control. In normal circumstances it was more an art than science, but low on fuel and with the cargo, both human and otherwise, poorly distributed due to the rushed entrance of the final and unexpected occupants, this landing would be like guiding an eighteen wheeler pulling a mobile home through a fast food drive thru. Further complicating matters was Senator Fillmore, who after a few hours in space had apparently determined he was an expert in flying rocket ships and gave a running dialog on which engine to fire, when and by how much.

As Boz managed to maneuver to the final position, it came spinning around on the side of space station. But it wasn't the docking hatch, but rather XJ3, wedged beneath XJ 4 with its tail section sticking out awkwardly and bearing down on XJ1.

"Watch out!" screamed the Senator, "Get us out of here!"

Hitting all four thrusters Boz easily pushed XJ1 out of the way, but in doing so, he saw as the lights for auxiliary engines three and four blinked red – out of fuel. Captain Boz snarled at the Senator, "Here we are, out of fuel, headed the wrong way, and two engines down. If we waited... and seen this... it'd be easy fix. Line it up for the next time around. But now..."

Looking completely guilty from his actions the Senator said in a miffed voice, "Well, we had to do something."

"Yeah, thanks to you… it might be die."

The Senator glanced over, his ego demanding a reply. In a rare instance, words escaped him.

Just One More Spin?

As Gordon and Manson arrived on the bridge, the men waiting for them seemed rather calm, positioned as if expecting their entrance. Gordon, not really a man of words, had a sense of nervousness come over him. What was he to do? Barely able to nod at Jim and Kevin. They didn't seem to notice his action, their attention focused on Manson. If they were looking for a hint as to what was to come, they were disappointed as Manson seemed stone faced.

Turning his attention to Gordon, Jim said in a voice hoping to earn a response, "Hello… Gordon is it? We've been waiting for you. Apparently you've something to tell us."

Averting his eyes, Gordon mumbled, "Well… er. I showed something to your man here."

"Really? Not a problem. I'll take the news from either. Doesn't matter." Smiling at Manson, Jim continued, "Sir. You have the floor so to speak. Inform me… inform us. What is the delicate issue we must address?"

Manson seemed only slightly more eager to talk than Gordon. Finally he began, "Well, ah… We got us a problem."

"So I hear. But so far no one will put it to words. It must be big, or that's the rumor."

"Yup. We gotta go back."

"Back?" Jim had determined despite what had recently happened that he would play this meeting cool, but he hadn't expected such a comment. "Manson, I mean… really… we can't."

"We gotta. It's the only way."

"No, we can't. There's nothing to go back to. The last rockets had to fight their way off the tarmac. Senator told me so himself. Quite literally. Brought up half the launch pad crew with him. Earth as we know it is no more. There is no way back."

"And we're not going back either," said Gordon firmly.

Smiling at Gordon, Jim said warmly, "No. I know of your situation. Of the list. That's been taken care of."

"How?"

"Well… XJ3. It arrived recently, everyone aboard dead."

"What? I don't believe you."

"Fine," said Jim casually and with confidence. Pointing a thumb out the window he said, "Take a look, any one you prefer. Their bodies are floating all about." Jim was rather proud of himself. He said the words calmly and with an even voice. No cracking or other signs of breaking down.

Gordon thrust himself toward the windows in the front, then one side, then the other. Sure enough, the space surrounding the ship showed bodies drifting along as if tied to the station by invisible lines.

"How?"

"Don't know really. Best guess… ran out of air. Whatever it was, they made a last desperate run."

Gordon nodded his head in understanding, then said softly, "Makes sense… I guess."

"So… Gordon, or Manson. Either one. I explained that fact to Gordon's wife Terri, and a man claiming to be Captain Majewski. They were for some reason sufficiently unimpressed by this fact. Wouldn't explain why. Said I had to talk to you. And I must confess, I don't know what could possibly exceed what we have floating about us."

Again Gordon nodded in agreement, but Manson only said, "We've got to go back. It's the only way."

Jim frowned at Manson, but quickly the expression was removed. He was long familiar with his stoic yet accurate assessments of situations. But the surprise was that Manson was always the one finding the solutions, figuring out things that couldn't otherwise be solved.

"We got to go back."

"Manson, that's not possible. We can't. There is no way. Earth is gone." Pointing out the window Jim said, "Go ahead… look." Framed in the window was Earth. But it wasn't the normal healthy blue and white seen in pictures. Rather it was blue and white but with a fiery jagged orange line down the middle. Manson glided over to the window, staring at the distant view of the Earth, lightly touching his fingers to the walls.

With his eyes fixed on the sight and with a face full of concentration he mumbled, "Got to be a way."

"So what is this? What's the problem?"

Still focused on Earth, Manson said in a soft voice, "Food. We got no food. Nothing on board."

Suddenly angry Gordon said, "That's not true! I showed you food."

"Ya… he did. Hardly a thing. Not enough."

Jim was trying to take in the meaning of all this. "No food. Little food? How much? We've got gardens as well you know."

"Nope," replied Manson, "No gardens. No dirt. No seeds. Just a small bit of frozen food in a food bin. Number one. All the rest… empty. We gotta go down. No other way."

"You sure? Manson… you got that right?"

"Walked the whole ship, stem to stern. Nothing. Plenty of water though. Just one trip down. That's all. We might starve trying then. But it's worth a shot."

"With what?" asked Gordon, "With what? They don't put extra fuel on these rockets. And are you familiar with how to return a rocket to earth?"

Tapping on the glass toward rocket ship XJ1 Manson said, "No, but I bet he is, whoever is flying that rocket."

"And if you land. *If* that is, how do you fill it with meals? And oh, get it back on the launching pad, load up with fuel, and take off."

"We left, didn't we? Just a short time ago."

"Manson," interrupted Jim, "It's changed since then. "

"But I'll bet he can fly us down there, land, and get us back."

"No food you say?" said Jim as he mulled the options, "Let's try this. Ok Manson, thanks. Can you please wait outside?" As Manson left Jim motioned for Gordon to close the door and opening the mike to XJ1 he asked, "Senator, you there?"

After a pause the response was, "Yeah. I'm here. You figure out how to get me on board yet?"

"You mentioned the situation on Earth before. Can you give me an update… some backfill."

With a tinge of frustration in his voice he said, "Earth? I told you. I need to get on board. We can't go back. Had to fight our way on the rocket, gunfire everywhere. They're shooting down the rockets on the pads and temperatures are soaring. There is no mission control. Can I make it any plainer to you. We need on there."

"But could you land back on Earth? If we took care of that, could you land?"

"Hell I don't know. I'm not a pilot."

"Let me speak to him, your Captain that is."

"Well… I don't see the point."

"Bear with me Senator, this might be the way to getting you on board."

Again there was a silence before Boz's voice could be heard saying, "Yeah?"

"Hello Captain, this is Jim LaBlanc."

"Hey, Captain Jay Boz here. What's up?"

"I have a question for you. Could you land your rocket ship back on Earth?"

"Could I… Huh? We just took off."

"Yes I know. But could you? Could you do it?"

"Right now… no. I got no fuel. We had to make an emergency launch and didn't get a full payload of fuel, just what they keep on board for such a situation. I'm down to the motion jets – got only two now – just used for docking and undocking. It's a miracle I got us here."

"But, if we got fuel. Could you land, load up, refuel, and take off?"

"Um… no. XJ2 was shot down, crashed on the landing strip. Even if we could, it takes a lot of fuel to land one of these things. Think about it, we're twice the size a 747 jumbo jet and you want to land on one point of land on Earth. That takes a lot of energy unless you are positioned just right. Why?"

"Just keeping options open. If you landed, what about reloading."

"Reload? What do you mean?"

"The process of reloading."

"Well, that's easy. There is nothing to reload. We haven't had shipment of anything in a week or so. Everyone quit or the payloads get hijacked. It's crazy out there. Worse even now. You know they got a tank on the tarmac? Last contact with mission control they were shooting up everything; fuel tanks, hangers, rockets, everything in sight. Again, say you could land and there was something to reload. To take off, you need a fuel payload… there's no fuel. You need to stand the rocket upright… mission control is gone and the machinery to do that shot to hell. And don't forget it's over two hundred degrees down there now, and rising. I heard it might reach three soon."

Frowning Jim said, "Ok, thanks."

Senator Fillmore, tired of these pointless details, said, "Ok Jim, let's talk about docking. Work on slowing that spin down a little more. Once the hatch comes around again. I'm coming in."

"No Senator, not yet."

"Hell yes Jim LaBlanc. I'm running this show, and when we come around again, I'm docking!"

Jim was going to object but realized that wouldn't work. Instead he did as a Chief of Staff is supposed to do, get information. "Ok Senator, when is that?"

"Don't know. We just missed it. Actually it's about to pass us by, but my damn Captain screwed everything up."

In the background there were some garbled words of protest as the Senator continued, "So when were in this position again, we will be docking."

Jim looked out the window and could see the Earth easily. Rather simple. He had to come up with a solution and rather quickly. He had one spin of the ship. When the Earth next came into view the Senator was going to try to board. Either he would be successful, damage the hull trying, or attach and rip the rocket and space station apart. There had to be a better solution.

Ennie Meanie Minnie Moe... Who Is To Die?

Jim typed into the keyboard, <<Met with Gordon. What do you propose?>>

<<Simple, we've already decided. No one is getting on board.>>

<<Who is this and who are we?>>

<<This is Captain Majewski and 'we' are Terri, Gordon, and I.>>

<<And that's all. Keep the Senator and the rest on the rocket from boarding?>>

<<No.>>

<<Inform me. I've been patient so far. What else?>>

<<Did Gordon tell you how many meals are on board?>>

<<Not exactly. We're short, and quite a bit.>>

<<10,000. That's all. For a three year trip.>>

<<And?>>

<<And we did the math. Everyone in dining room B will survive.>>

Jim stared blankly at the words on the screen. He and his children were in dining room B. But Olga? His wife was still in dining room A. Stalling for time he typed, <<Two hundred people, 10000 meals…>>

"Say Kevin, you any good with math? What's ten thousand divided by two hundred."

"Let's see ten thousand divided by two, that's five thousand… knock off two zeros… equals fifty."

Jim typed, <<That's 50 meals per person total. You can make that last three years?>>

Finally came the response. <<This is Terri. I told you it was horrible.>>

<<Sure is, that's suicide.>>

<<No, it's not. Please don't make me type it. Even now I don't approve.>>

What could it be? Then Kevin said, "My god. They want us to eat each other."

Jim had lost his composure when watching the people float out of the hatch to die. He was determined not to do so again. Instead he bit his lip so hard he could taste blood. Were they serious? They wanted… they were going to kill and eat everyone in dining room A.

<<Are you mad?>> he typed without even realizing it.

<<No. This is Captain Majewski. As I said, already decided, run the numbers. It is the only way.>>

<<No. you can't. There's got to be another way.>>

<<Let's be honest. We've already done this exact same thing, and recently. We allowed everyone on Earth to die. All of them. Any one of us could have given up our spots, yet we're all here. This is no different.>>

But it was to Jim. Before he was making decisions in order to save his family. Now Olga was to be chopped up and served for dinner... to his children no less. Quite a different matter.

His stomach beginning to turn Jim typed, <<I need some time>> and he spun away from the computer screen, as if that would remove this problem.

Now in front of him he saw Gordon, who was peering deeply at him, trying to read his mood. Finally he said in a flat but concerned voice, "You don't know me, but I'm an engineer. A practical sort of guy. And from my perspective, it's simple math."

"Simple math? Locking people away to kill them... so that you can live? This isn't like Earth. I never picked who died. Those of us who are on board, we found a way for ourselves."

"It's no different."

"Yes it is. In one you are trying to survive, the other is no less than genocide."

"Consider it this way. It's like losing weight."

"Losing weight? We're not going on a diet. We are herding people apart and slaughtering them like old horses."

Without pausing Gordon continued, "All diets, no matter the ingredients, come down to the same formula. How many calories you take in, and how many you work off. No matter the diet... that's the ultimate result. That's a fact. Only in this case... where we are right now, it's not a question of how to lose weight, but how many calories to survive on, and divide that into how many calories are available. We only have so many calories on board."

"But we…" That was all Jim could get out. His mind was racing, wondering how long before the ship could spin and dock with the Senator. They might then be able to get control of the ship's computer again. And then another thought came thundering into his mind… that meant bringing more people on board. More people they couldn't feed. That would only exasperate the problem. And that meant the Senator would be on board. While Pitts and Lipscomb were possibly dead, the Senator had more such toughs brought along for security, and the Senator wouldn't be nearly as humanitarian as Jim was. Why, would Jim even make the cut of those who survived if the Senator was on board? Would any of his family for that matter?

Then he realized… quite naturally and without any shock. He was coming over to the idea that some would have to die… it was a question of who. Immediately the name of Senator Fillmore went to the top of the death list. After all, he wasn't on board. Frowning Jim recalled the insult presented to him. It was no coincidence that Jim was on the first rocket. The ship of the lower class, those expected to toil and work for others. In fact Jim barely knew any of the people on XJ1, the Senator included. Certainly none were the kind who could be considered friends, or even friendly. No, the Senator and all the others on XJ1 would not be boarding… at least not now. Having temporarily decided the fate of XJ1, it was time to feel out the determination of this Captain Majewski.

He typed, <<You know I can open a hatch and kill us all?>>

The response was immediate. <<And I can kill everyone in dining rooms A and B right now. Don't threaten me. We've already puzzled this out and moved everyone to dining room B. They will live. I need to know you are on board with this.>>

Hell no he wasn't. Till death do us part. For better or worse. Those were more than just words, more than vows. It was something he was determined to uphold, no matter what. He wasn't going to leave Olga to die... ground up into hamburger patties for the pleasure of others. How far had the space center spun? Earth was no longer visible in the window. He still had time to work this out before the Senator attempted to board.

<<Explain to me. Who is to live and why? I get the children, why the others?>>

<<Better to not ask me, mostly people Terri knew, like you, or had some sort of talent. Pulled records from the ship's registry. Let Terri go through the list.>>

After a pause Terri began to began to type in the listing of those selected and why. As Jim read the text, Kevin leaned over to Jim and whispered in his ear, "We got a problem."

Glancing at Kevin for only a moment before returning to the screen Jim said nothing. Kevin whispered, "My wife. She's on XJ1."

Again Jim bit his lip to control his emotions. He liked Kevin, what he knew of him. He was a military contractor, or some such thing. Had even met his wife. She'd recently been hired on the Senator's staff, against Jim's wishes. She was pushy, aggressive, and not exactly trustworthy. In her short time with the Senator he'd already had three separate blowups between her and other staff members as she fought for more turf. Her behavior reminded him of the worst side of Senator Fillmore. Jim now could actually observe in his mind... how the emotions were changing. It was the way he was, what made him a great Chief of Staff. Because of that he seemed almost a spectator as his mind churned through the facts. In this case it was Kevin's comment, carving it up, analyzing it, and out spit the answer as if on a piece of paper. He didn't like her, didn't like the Senator. Neither were people of any character. The rocket would not dock and they would not be boarding. They would die.

Again he glanced at Kevin and with his best expressionless face nodded to show he understood. Smiling grimly Kevin said, "I didn't think we'd leave any of this up to these idiots. We'll do what's necessary? Once she's on board, we can work all this out."

Jim nodded back. Of course he would. He just wouldn't say that as far as he was concerned, in this case… necessary was to keep Kevin's wife off the space station, her and the remainder of the passengers of XJ1. Returning to reading the descriptions of those in dining room B as they scrolled onto the screen, Jim wondered, how long would he have to make such ugly decisions… and be so secretive about the results? He frowned at the screen. Possibly for the rest of his life, however long that was. The life he knew, the one he grew up with and had lived… gone, never to return. It was a new world, or rather a life without Earth. That was fine. He'd do what he had to and become what was necessary to keep his family alive. After all, he was Jim LeBlanc, Chief of Staff. That came with the job description.

Muffin and Cupcake? Prepare to Board!

The Senator had been a lot of things in his life. There's no reason to print all of the many and varied descriptions of what those who knew him thought. A complementary description would have been, "Masterful head of the Ways and Means committee. Silver tongued and able to build coalitions that were stable and reliable." Despite the opinions of others regarding his personal life, as a legislator he was in his element. Gently twisting arms, cutting back room deals, yet always with his eye on the ultimate goal being accomplished.

As a person? He was a distant but loving father, rather normal for someone in his position. He could show great kindness and even greater savagery as is the personality of a politician. And of course along with great power develops a great ego. He had never been President nor would he. He didn't have that sheen of success they typically had. His suits were rumpled, hair mussed, and felt no internal need to give speeches. But it was power enough to grow the ego that now wanted more. For him, while the earth was still viable, the only next step up was President. But as the ecological disaster unfolded and air temperatures rose, he began to see what he quickly determined was his destiny. He would be the one to lead earthlings, the entire civilization of Earth for that matter, to safety. He had been put in the position to select the best of the planets, the best of the space ships, the best of the plant and animal life. And as a reward for doing this job with his natural efficiency… it became clear that as a reward for hard work executed at the highest level, he would be the leader of New Earth.

Let's be clear on this. The Senator was a loyal American. He supported the constitution, defending it against all enemies. But… to be so close to the actual root threads of power. Wouldn't it have all been so much easier without all this? No elections, no parties, no running for office. He had been to Communist China on many occasions and though he never would admit to it, he secretly had was he called "communist envy." The desire to weld power without any sharing, questions, or interruption. Of course that would never happen… not on Earth… not in the United States.

But on New Earth? This was his chance, his one opportunity. Could he be like Caesar? The man who overthrew the Roman Republic and caused the birth of the Empire? Could Senator Fillmore lead a small group of Americans to a new planet and build a society based upon the morals, precepts, and beliefs of America… with one major difference? No elected government. New Earth would function as ancient Rome. A small collection of connected families ruling over the masses, of course with the Fillmore clan holding the anointed seat of the highest of the high.

It was all too simple. He had total control over the activities of SS 221 and SS 222 and their related rockets. He had even sent his second son, Lanny, on the small one person space ship that left earlier for New Earth and held a water converter. The piece of equipment that was to convert the barren desert like planet into a virtual paradise. Every person, plant, and animal had been personally approved by the Senator. While others made virtual worlds with pigs and cows, he was going to do it real live beings, cramming them into two massive space stations and carting them off to a distant planet.

As for the people? This too would be much like Rome. Sophisticated, educated, intellectual. But also not so pious, fake and shallow as people pretended to be. If there was a way to sum up his society, it would have been patterned after the old playboy television show hosted by Hugh Heffner, with the Senator filling in the magazine mogul's role. As for how he would rule, he'd made a simple decision. At first he would have to be a dictator. After all, their small group would be it… possibly all of human society in one small ship. Any loss of control could be catastrophic. And that meant hiring on men such as Admiral Pitts, Captain Lipscomb, and others like them. They knew how to take control and were willing to follow orders, no matter where they were led. Of course that would be very helpful once the small colony was established on New Earth. He would not stand for any revolt or challenge to his power, nor of his behavior.

Needless to say, in reviewing the history and personality of the Senator, there was an alternate view. In short he was considered to be a jerk. A liar, fraud, and manipulator. The type of man who when authorized to select those granted access onto SS 222, picked three girlfriends in addition to his wife, his only regret was those female companions left behind. His drinking habit was legendary, as were the charges of improper activity he'd managed to fight off and squelch. Brawls, strippers, and a variety of drunken misdemeanors related to his behavior. And what was the Senator's opinion of all that? Proud of it and would do it again in a heartbeat. He had a wife of course… a requirement for public office. But she had long ago been dismissed from such consideration for that in anything other than title by the Senator a long time ago.

As to divorce, that had been considered and deemed inconvenient. It would cost him money, an embarrassing trial, and do nothing for his career. Not to mention it was easy to put off questions of marriage by his variety of female companions with the simple reply, "I'm married already." Still there were occasional prices to be paid for his behavior, and now the time was arriving to pay the toll once again. Determined to dock with SS 222 when the hatch came around next, word was sent to his wife that her presence was requested. He had promised, she would be the first to alight onto the space station from their rocket and was intent to keep the commitment.

As she floated into the captain's chamber, her two precious pets were clutched in her arms. Muffin and Cupcake, teacup sized Shih Tzu dogs that she wore almost as if earrings or other jewelry. Once a true natural beauty… age, drink, and too many rich foods had turned her frumpy, wrinkled, and worn around the edges. She had overlooked the affairs, bad behavior, and rude comments in exchange for moments like this. On Earth, everyone she had known was on the verge of an unpleasant death. But not Dolly. She was on XJ1 with her beloved mother and cherished children all aboard on XJ2… save Lanny.

As she arrived the Senator said, "Alright Dolly. I said you'd be the first, and so it will be."

She nodded and smiled brightly at the Senator, possibly for the first time in who knew how long.

"The hatch is just behind you, right outside the Captain's cabin that we're in now.

"Ok," she said in her high sweet voice.

"And don't worry, I'll be right behind you." There was a time when those words would have been considered a comfort. But now it was simply part of the polite banter they had chosen over the screaming matches they had involved in for so many years. All Dolly Fillmore cared about was getting on SS 222 and their new destination. Although older, her mother hen instincts were still quite functional and she couldn't wait to create a nest on New Earth.

"And when will we be boarding?"

"Soon. Very soon. But we have a short wait ."

Dolly adjusted her hold on Muffin and Cupcake, causing one of the dogs to give out a protesting, "Ruff!" She didn't like waiting. She was the wife of a Senator. Waiting was not something she was accustomed to or approved of. So she gave what she called her five minute expression. It meant that of course she could wait... for five minutes. A look the Senator knew very well and ignored. Yet another reason for the informal dissolution of their once happy marriage.

Two Jacks And A Joker

Kevin had been sent to docking room one, presumably the Senator would be attempting to latch onto the space station. Jim wanted to make sure everything was proper so that when they docked – if that was possible – all of the necessary equipment was up and ready. Well... that was what Kevin was told, certain that would keep him occupied. Once Kevin was dispatched, he set up a meeting with the Triumvirate currently ruling the space station; Terri, Gordon, and Captain Majewski. Even in space it seemed; a negotiation was a negotiation.

It took some convincing, but finally they agreed to meet in the intersection of the food bins, apparently far from their current hiding place, and allowed Jim to possibly see in person if Admiral Pitts and Captain Lipscomb were in fact dead. As he approached the meeting location, Gordon followed along. A concession he made to show that he was not trying to take over the informal leadership.

Upon arriving a young, thin man known who must be the one calling himself Captain Majewski said bruskly, "Ok, you wanted to see us. Here we are."

Jim smiled. Never show your cards, it is bad form. "You said you could show me where the Admiral and Lipscomb are."

"Sure. Bin 200. Right over there."

Jim glanced over where the Captain had pointed. Then gliding to the food bin, he taped the outer surface with the palm of his hand lightly. "Dead?"

"If not now… then soon."

Jim nodded as if an expert on such things as freezing people to death. Then holding a hand up to rap on the door he asked, "Do you mind?"

"Naw. They can't get out."

Jim knocked his knuckles on the door as hard as he could several times. There was no response. He looked at the Captain who said, "Most likely."

"Or there's no one in there."

The Captain frowned, then glared over at Terri, before pushing over to the freezer door. The temperature gauge said negative forty degrees. Apparently it was easy in the cold of space to cool things down.

"Can you open it?"

"I can, why?"

"Because I want to see the truth of your words."

The Captain stared at the door. There were three of them, and only one of him. It would be easy to overpower Jim and shove him in. It would make their life much easier. But guessing what he was thinking, Gordon said from behind, "Don't worry, I won't toss you in. Won't let them either."

"Yes," said Terri, "In fact before you open it, we have to agree, if they try to get out, you won't help them."

As the Captain looked around Jim said, "See there? We're already becoming friends. Not close ones, not yet I think. But it's a good bet for you. What do you say?"

"I'm not sure they're dead."

"Were they wearing any special clothing?"

"No."

"Well then. Negative forty. I'd think that it wouldn't take long for them to expire."

The Captain glanced around. Why possibly let these dangerous men out. Their fate was sealed. He decided to compromise. "Tell you what. Let's talk. You let me in on how you see things. And then... we'll see about opening the door."

Staring at the door Jim said, "Fair enough."

"Ok. What you got?"

Jim looked around, trying to determine the best way to begin. "We have as you know a situation. Rather a standoff if you will."

"How's that?"

"You have dining room A on lock down. I have a whole host of people who want to come on board."

Sounding as if he'd been threatened, the Captain said, "So you want to bring them on board do you?"

"Please... let me finish. I think my intention will be very clear if you do."

Jim waited to see if the Captain had more to say, when greeted with silence, he continued, "As I said, we have different grips on this state of affairs. Then throw in the limited number of meals, and we have a combustible situation. Decisions must be, and in fact have been. I couldn't agree more with the selection of the children."

Jim paused to see if his complement had any effect, but while Terri and Gordon perked up at the comment, the Captain still seemed moody and out of sorts.

"As for the remained of those selected, I agree as well. Good decisions, or well enough. One really won't know until they are put to action." Again he paused, but the Captain showed no improvement in mood.

"But I do have one adjustment to make. It will keep all of your decisions in place and I think improve all of our lives for the trip." He paused, waiting for an answer.

"Go on," instructed the Captain, already expressing a sour face over the proposition.

Moving his eyes from one to the other of his audience, Jim said, "I'm recommending we add ten people to the list of those who live."

"Ten!" started the Captain.

"Oh come on now," said Gordon, "The number we came up with…"

At least he had one supporter, as Terri grinned at the thought.

"I know. It was done with a little fat in it, maybe more. But we've got to."

"Why?" asked the Captain.

"To keep the peace."

"Peace? What peace? We've got all the peace you can imagine here. That's the point of the two hundred."

"Let me put it this way. I'm willing to go to bat for you. Do something I hate to, that none of you want to. But in exchange for my loyalty, there is a price."

"Like what?"

"There is a man named Kevin. He made you're list as one of your technical people. I've no problem with that. But it seems his wife... she is on XJ1."

That brought a silence over the group. The initial decisions had been made on functionality and Terri only knew of her coworkers in the professional sense. It never occurred that they might have other relations on board.

"Think about it," said Jim, "Killing someone's loved one... might cause some dysfunction."

"Yeah, I can see that."

"So I've got a list. Ten people. Five percent increase. Not too much I think. And in exchange, I'll take care of Senator Fillmore and XJ1."

"What do you mean?"

"I mean, he plans to force his way onto this ship, and the next chance he has at the docking station is when. We're slowly spinning toward that point now. I'll go to the docking station and lock it out. Whatever it takes."

"Can't," said the Captain, "It doesn't have a lock on it."

"Well then, what does it have?"

"Only this. If it has a leak or some other problem, there is a manual override. Pull the level, it releases the locks holding the rocket in place, and uses a piston to push the docking rocket away. But they have to dock before you can do that."

"There need to be a leak to be active?"

"No. That's why it's a manual override. Just in case."

"Ok. I'll do it. But in return. I've got a list. Ten people."

"And if we don't?"

"You seem strong enough, but you've seen Kevin. Also we have Manson. Four of us, and Manson is in excellent shape. We defend the dock. The Senator gets on. And we take it from there."

After a pause the Captain asked, "And who are they? These ten additions?"

"Family members of those already selected. Almost all of them."

"And why not fifteen. We have fifteen adults."

"Some aren't married, or I don't know what they are. Right now I'm not about to take a census."

The Captain glanced at Gordon and Terri. He had privately committed to not allowing any more discussions of such things with the Johnsons, considering how with their two votes to his one, they had him at a disadvantage on the original selections. "No," he announced, "We can't get them out. Thin chef, he warned everyone. We open the door and we're done for."

Jim smiled. Sometimes he didn't like how clever, and underhanded he could be. "I can get them out."

"How?"

"Leave that to me. I guarantee. We can get them."

"No. Trusting Gordon and Terri got you in the mix. I sure didn't pick you."

"Hey come on now," said Terri defensively, "We did pretty darn good. Jim's going to take care of the Senator. What more can you ask for?"

The Captain bit his lip. She was right, he had overstepped his bounds. "Sorry," he said softly, "But if we don't know how you are going to do it. Then the answer is no."

Jim looked at the others, then nodded in agreement. "Fair enough." Reaching into a pocket he pulled out a walkie-talkie. It was the one concession the Senator had given him in exchange for going on board XJ4. "Olga, has one as well."

"Who's Olga?"

"My wife. One of the ten."

And she's…"

"In dining room A. She knows everyone on the list, or I can point her to them."

"And from there?"

"Easy, there are several doors to the dining room. Herd them toward one. Unlock it, they slip out, Olga let's me know, and boom... the doors are locked again. Can you do just that? Unlock just one door?"

It had been simple to the Captain. No additions to the list. But now in the moment, he needed advice. Despite his concerns, he glanced at Terri and Gordon.

Terri's smile easily expressed her position. But Gordon? He was thinking hard. It was an ugly deal. What if food was already short? But then, this would keep the Senator and all XJ1 off of the space station. A small increase considering how many they had already selected. It was a good deal, and he indicated so with the slightest of nods.

"Done," said the Captain, closing a deal.

"Good," said Jim, "Now. Let's see what you've got in that freezer.

The Captain frowned, but a deal was a deal. How would they keep those three men at bay if they were still alive? Two were military men, and the third huge... even if fat.

Sliding to the lock, he inserted the key and released it. Pulling the shaft from the door, he hesitated, as if waiting a moment or so might end their lives.

Then he slowly opened the door and a brace of cold air hit them. Three men were in the middle of the freezer. They had wrapped their arms around each other to keep warm in a futile effort to survive. With pale skin and dilated pupils, they were deep into the stages of hypothermia or gone.

"Dead," said the Captain.

"Possibly," said Jim, "Or hibernation."

"Then we can save them?" asked Terri hopefully.

"No," said Jim with finality. He was a card player and often played games that used only part of the deck. And as he looked at the three men frozen in mid embrace, they looked like large, frozen, animated playing cards. The two military men reminded him of Jacks, and the fat chef, complete with his tall chef's hat, seemed the motley Joker card. Two Jacks and a Joker. Strange game they were playing. Jacks almost always were kept, not so much with Jokers. Either way it didn't matter. Jim was about to toss out the King.

Closing the door Jim said, "They'd be most desirable if on our side. Hate to say it, but both are very dangerous to us." And internally he added, "And would take a spot for my Olga."

Who did that leave? What did he think of this three headed monster that was deciding the fate of who would live and who would die? As he looked from Gordon to Terri to Captain Majewski, his trained eye made an assessment. Smart fellow this Gordon. But he was as he described himself. An engineer. Dull and plain. A numbers guy. And Terri? Clever, efficient… a hard worker. Already knew that. Can never have enough of her type. But nothing to build upon.

Then his eye fell upon Captain Majewski. Lean and wiry, he had a glint in his eye… determination. Ready for battle and showed he was up to the challenge. He had wanted to see the bodies of the Admiral and Lipscomb. Those were hardened warriors. Not easy for anyone to kill, yet he had seen them, frozen and locked away like slabs of beef. This was a long trip, and Jim LaBlanc was no leader. Power behind the throne? Yes, he could be that, and easily so. It was what he was made for. He decided to make a test. Extending a hand he said, "Ok… Captain Majewski." The handshake was firm and confident. One never knew of such things. Many the coward knew how to impress, but it was a good start. Now if only he did as well with keeping XJ1 from docking, things would be all the more better.

No Docking Zone

Jim was finally heading down the hallway toward the XJ1 docking station after spending extra time in the narrow hallway that accessed the nuclear reactors, using the backup computer to review how the locking and releasing mechanism worked when disconnecting XJ1. It wasn't the complexity of the task, they would have only one chance at this. If the Senator managed to get on the space station, there was always the possibility of a negotiation, or possibly a simple matter of stuffing him into a food bin, freezing him to icicles. But more likely it would result in a swarm of the Senator's loyalists pouring onto the space station, forcing Jim to cede control to the Senator. Once the food situation was discovered, that would most likely mean a death sentence for all currently on board, possibly with the courtesy of a brief trial, but more likely the result of a lynch mob.

All this could be avoided by preventing the Senator and his allies on XJ1 from breaching the hull. The easiest would be to for Captain Boz of XJ1 to fail in his attempt to dock with SS 222, held at bay either due to the space station's rotation or stopped by a lack of fuel. Although Jim wasn't an expert on the difficulties of guiding rocket ships, he was already impressed by Captain Boz's ability to reach his destination, despite minimum fuel levels and a mistimed launch. He was likely, as were all of the Senator's selections, top notch. If it was possible to dock, Jim was confident Captain Boz would manage the feat. That meant it would be up to him to disengage XJ1 once it docked, and preferably do so without Kevin knowing his motives. Jim doubted Kevin would be happy with his wife's death and apparently had independently come to the conclusion that the Senator would save both Kevin and Jim from extinction. Something Jim saw no reason to believe.

Regarding wives, Jim was on his walkie-talkie, clicking the Morse code button. Over and over again he thumbed the button three times. He wasn't an expert on such things, but he and Olga had worked out simple patterns. One beep was, "How are you?" Two beeps, "I'm fine." And three beeps, "Emergency." But he couldn't get a response. Reaching the edge of the docking station, he told Gordon to enter. This conversation needed to be done away from Kevin. One never knows the moods of men when their wives are involved and if Kevin found out Jim was saving the life of his wife while simultaneously terminating Kevin's spouse… people have killed for less. And that didn't mention the fact he included Kent Brooks, his nephew, on the list of the ten to be rescued. Such nepotism might cause trouble later, but better to be saved now than morn his premature and unnecessary death.

In mid thought, the list of the ten lucky to be saved was now upped by one… to eleven to include Crystal Flats, one of the Senator's girlfriends. A raven haired beauty, Jim was already slotting her as the future spouse for Kevin. A Chief of Staff has to be planning several moves ahead of everyone else, and Jim was already calculating that with his wife gone, Kevin would have slim pickings for a replacement. And it didn't hurt that Jim found her a devastating beauty. After all, what would one woman hurt? If it was to be only two hundred some odd people that survived, they might as well have at least one good looking women to appreciate.

First, the process of segregating the eleven from the others had to begin. Again he beeped the walkie-talkie three times. This time he got a response. What he had hoped for was the agreed upon three beeps, followed by Olga finding a private corner of dining room A to communicate. Instead he got an excited Olga loudly stating, "Goot god Jimmie! They meant to kilt us, kilt us all!"

Jim cringed at the words. Maybe it wasn't such a good idea to have married the emotional Olga; a gorgeous blonde Swede he stumbled across while on a trip to Europe. Such are the follies of youth. Again the walkie-talkie was beeped three times, hoping this would cause his wife to realize they needed to speak in private. But instead the response – received in high volume – was a frantic, "Jimmie! Jimmie! Wit are all here! Come to us... save us. Save us all!" This time he stared at the walkie-talkie dumbfounded. She was the mother of his children and a loving wife. But sometimes... drama queen. What was he to do? Leave her to die? For a moment in his frustration, he thought maybe. No, she was his wife and he would save her.

Moving even further from the docking area, he made the decision and pressing on the button said, "Olga, it's me."

"Oh mite got! Jimmie. Wit are loct in here! There is mad men running about, trying to take over. Listen!" She held the walkie-talkie in the air so that everyone might shout, which of course with her encouragement they all did.

"Olga? Olga!"

When a voice responded, it wasn't Olga, but Barry Wilson, who had apparently snatched the walkie-talkie from Olga. He was a pushy sort, bombastic and arrogant... not to mention very large, announcing on the walkie-talkie, "This is Barry! Who am I speaking with?"

"Damn it! Give that back to Olga! Now!"

"No! I'm in charge here."

"The hell you are! When I hear Olga, I'll speak again! Everyone hear that?"

The walkie-talkie went silent. Jim was willing to wait until that occurred when in the distance Jim heard Gordon say, "Here it comes. Jim, get in here!" Snapping the power off he hurried to the docking area, he saw Kevin on his right manning the controls operating a mechanical arm attached to the outside the space station. It was designed to grab the rocket and pull it into the position. Ten feet away and by the docking door was Gordon, both hands on the lever to activate the manual override. It was a simple operation. If XJ1 managed to properly dock Gordon would snatch the lever down and Jim would press the button releasing the locks and activating the exit piston, which Gordon was supposed to have adjusted to maximum strength.

"Gordon... we ready?" asked Jim.

Gordon responded with a grim faced nod which Jim took to imply the piston was properly adjusted. A glance out the window showed XJ1 quite a distance away. With the rear thruster engines apparently empty, Captain Boz was firing both of the forward engines, sending the rocket spinning sideways towards the space station as it began to approach. As it spun about, the rocket closed in on the space station, and Jim watched with awe, it was like throwing a dart across a room and hitting a target falling to the ground... and expecting to hit not just the bulls eye, but a perfect one. As the rear of the rocket swung past the space station Jim braced for the impending impact. It occurred to him that the force of the blow of the rocket might solve everyone's problems, smashing a hole in the side of the space station and killing everyone.

As the front of the rocket came into sight, Jim could see the Captain furiously working the angles of the thruster rockets as he tried to angle the hatch to the docking door. Every second or so, one of the maneuvering jets tilted to a new angle before firing orange jets of flames. With a crash, XJ1's hatch slammed into the docking door, clicking down and locking. A perfect fit. The impact sent Kevin, Gordon, and Jim sailing away as the outer hull partially crumpled and space station's outer hatch popped off the hull, sailing inside the room. Kevin bounced off the wall to the docking room and was now upside down. Taking advantage of Kevin's disorientation, Jim shoved Kevin away from the controls to the mechanical arm.

Almost immediately the door to the rocket opened and there, eyes open as wide as possible was the Senator's Fillmore's wife, Dolly. First Cupcake, and then Muffin made a nervous, "Ruff!" Or was it Muffin who spoke first? It was impossible to tell unless you knew the color of the ribbon they always wore on their bodies. Muffin wore blue and Cupcake red, or was it the other way? Then a voice from behind snarled, "Damn it Dolly! Move your fat ass!" It was the Senator who presumably shoved her from behind through the small round hatch doorway. Shoving himself forward toward the opening Jim shouted, "The seal, it's leaking!" Reaching the manual override lever he ripped it downward, but it jammed halfway down.

Diving under the entering Dolly Fillmore Jim pushed her at Kevin to obstruct his view. Kevin screamed, "No! We can get them on board!" The button for the emergency release piston was now partially uncovered from its protective casing and Jim smashed his hand toward it. He could feel as a finger bent awkwardly from the action, but other fingers reached it, tapping the button. It wasn't enough, and as Jim raised his hand to see his middle finger bent backwards Gordon shoved him away and reaching down pushed hard on the button. There was a sudden shuddering as the piston tried to push through the space station's damaged hull. Slowly it moved out as the screeching of the metal piston on the torn hull could be heard. Then suddenly the piston freed and slammed into the rocket, pushing away the rocket's hatch, along with the space station's still attached hull, which began to rip away.

First Jim shoved Dolly out of the docking room, sending her cartwheeling from the room. As she released Muffin and Cupcake they sailed through the door behind her like two furry baseballs. Grabbing Gordon, Jim announced, "It's tearing, we've got to get out." As the Piston continued to push forward it swung the body of the rocket ship away from the space station, continuing to tear the hatch from SS 222., along with part of the space ship itself.

Screaming, "NO!" Kevin shoved himself toward the rocket ship, cramming the Senator back inside, trying to see his wife. As the hatch door tore completely from the space station, air from the space station assisted in pushing the rocket away. Jim and Kevin darted from the room, closing the doorway to the docking room and sealing it. Seeing the stunned faces of Gordon and Dolly, Jim said, "Don't worry, these ships are designed like that. " The only response was a pair of confused, "ruffs!" from Cupcake and Muffin who floated about Dolly's head like oversized flies, one curled up as if being held while the other ran in mid air, trying futilely to reach its master.

10000 Meals

Returning to the bridge with Gordon, Jim typed the message, <<It's done. Stopped the Senator. Please come to the bridge.>>

Instead of a quick agreement, the response was a terse, <<How do we know?>>

This was quickly followed by, <<Is Gordon there?>>

Once, <<Yes,>> was typed in, <<What is our son's middle name and how did we select that?>>

Gordon leaned over the keyboard and typed, <<Harris. Your maiden name.>>

This was followed after a pause by, <<Is it true? Was the Senator stopped?>>

Gordon typed, <<Yes. Best we could for now.>>

<<Ok. We'll be there.>>

It wasn't long before Captain Majewski and Terri arrived. As they entered Jim stated, "It's done. The Senator won't be docking."

"How do you know?"

"He ripped the docking room to pieces."

Both the Captain and Terri looked shocked at the comment.

"And the ship? Did it occur to you we might need it intact?"

"Yup. The best I could do."

"He's right," said Gordon, "Did our best. Their Captain, did a hell of a job to dock. Took everything we could to disengage."

Then, slyly glancing over at the still upset Captain, Jim said softly, "Um. We picked up another passenger... three in fact."

"Three!"

"Aw no, he's joking," interrupted Gordon, "Picked up one. She had two dogs with her. Tiny as could be."

"So we picked up... one?"

"Yup. The Senator's wife."

"That's still one too many. How'd she get on board?"

"Like I said, we did what we could. She came on board when they docked, but we got rid of the rest."

"And they are?"

"Still out there, but I doubt they have much if any fuel," said Jim.

"How's that?"

"As they came in, only had two ancillary jets working, and one… as they approached, seemed to flame out."

"So… he's got an engine left?"

"One with fuel. And the docking door is ruined. I guess he could try to dock at one of the other two open docks."

"Nope. Each rocket is programmed for a specific door."

"Really, kinda stupid. Don't you think?"

"Not normally. They can be reprogrammed. But we're the only ones who can do that. So they can try to dock, but it's like an electronic key. If we don't change it to match the hatch for XJ1, they can't get in."

"Not unless they try smashing in, like they did this time."

"Really?"

"Why you think the docking room is destroyed? They came in as hot as possible."

"Wow."

"Wow is right, but that's been taken care of, just like I said I would. And oh, by the way. Kevin's wife is on board XJ1, so what I've told you. This goes no further than here."

This was the kind of secret dealings none wanted, and each took the news differently. Terri was crestfallen on the thought she was keeping a wife from her husband. Meanwhile Gordon, while appearing upset, showed his pragmatic side, showing little outwardly regarding this information. Jim was Jim, a bureaucrat who saw life in terms of a string of never ending deals. One simply made the best deal possible each time, hoping the overall sum of decisions would result in a better society. As for XJ1, Jim wasn't happy with refusing entry to XJ1, but was comfortable knowing they had done what was necessary.

And the Captain? No remorse, none at all. To him, the Senator was an enemy. There were too many mouths to feed, and the Senator had the power to send the Captain back to Earth. His steely look told everyone he approved of Jim's actions. After all, worse decisions were ahead. If they fell to pieces now, what would they do going forward? The Captain had already moved on.

Jim had been very clear. He would remove the Senator, and had for the most part. But with that success came the other side of the bargin. Ten more mouths to feed. And how the hell were they to get them out of dining room A? Jim said he had a plan. He better, cause Captain Majewski wasn't about to jeopardize the lives of everyone so that Jim LaBlanc could enjoy the company of his wife. Still a deal was a deal, now it was time for Jim to collect on the Captain's promise.

Turning to the Captain, Jim smiled. "We have an agreement, do we not?"

Frowning, Captain Majewski said, "Yes... we do."

"And have I not produced to your satisfaction?"

"Yes, so far."

"So, I say we work on my side of the deal. Once I get everything set up, you open the door. Everyone is ushered out, the door closed, and then…" His words trailed off. And then everyone remaining in dining room A would die. It was one thing to fend off the hostile and aggressive Senator Fillmore. It was another to treat people like cattle. Especially cattle headed for the slaughter. But after a brief silence, reality began to push against them, as it had been ever since learning of the food situation. The cold fact was that before takeoff the ship had to be placed into a state where all the stowage had been balanced out. And to do that, dining room A had to be… there was no easy way to say it. The contents of dining room A would have to be removed and placed in the food bins so that the ship was in balance. Had to be done. No other way. And to do that, everyone in dining room A had to be killed.

The Captain broke the silence with, "And how do you propose we proceed?"

"For you, it is simple. Once I select the door, you unlock it. We will assist them out, you relock it."

"And how are you going to get the ten segregated from the others?"

"I'm working on that. I need a quiet room and some time."

"We don't have much of that. Those people are hungry, locked down, and think they are battling a mutiny."

"Yes," said Jim with some frustration, "I'm aware of that. You don't have to remind me."

"Well it's the truth, isn't it?"

"Yes, it is," he said in a more agreeable tone, "You are correct. When we do this, I suggest you have your schedule down pat."

"I think we should be at the door," said Gordon.

"Why?"

"Muscle."

"Muscle?"

"Yeah. Muscle. We're already at capacity. If we take on ten more, that's a lot. But it might get ugly. I'll help at the door."

"Yes," said Jim, "When the time comes, I'll do the same."

"And Kevin."

"No. He's… I would guess unfit as of right now."

Gordon nodded in understanding. "So when?"

"Soon."

"Alright," said Captain Majewski, "How exactly are you going to do that? Walkie-talkie's are not exactly the most secret of communications. I'd hate to think of what would happen if they found out about that."

"Yes," said Jim, "That would be a problem. Well let me go. I need some quiet to do this."

"Why sneak off? I'd like to hear this. If we're to help, we should hear what's going on."

Jim was desperately trying to come up with a reason not to. It would be horrible if they found out the walkie-talkie had not only been discovered, but taken away. He wouldn't be surprised if Captain Majewski called the whole thing off. But after some mumbled complaints, he glanced around. It had to be done. Sometimes you had to roll the dice, and this was one of them, even with his wife's life was on the line.

Staring down at the walkie-talkie as he turned on the volume dial, the distinct 'click" was followed by a distant buzz. Then… before he could make a comment, the oversized voice of Barry Wilson came thundering over the walkie-talkie speaker, "Who the hell is on now! Talk to me! We demand to be heard!" Instinctively Jim clicked the walkie-talkie off, when he glanced up, he could see the angry faces of the Terri and Gordon, topped off by Captain Majewski who's purple face appeared ready to explode.

Trying weakly to change the subject, Jim addressed the new entrant to the bridge with, "Oh Molly, there you are."

The Lioness

As Dolly floated into the room – dogs clawed onto her shoulders – she gave the appearance of some strange three headed space monster. Her hair, originally rolled into large curls, had raised about her head in dark tentacles with streaks of grey and the frumpy dress had billowed out to make her seem three times her normal weight. She responded, "Jim," in that quiet voice she always used. The one that when angered got even quieter. "What is the situation?"

"Well, we've only got ten thousand meals on board."

Without hesitation Dolly said, "Goodness, a lot of people are going to have to die. Explain further. You've of course quarantined those who won't be making the trip? But I sense some sort of difficulty." That in summation was Dolly. Jim had given her but one sentence of information and already she had assessed the situation, come up with solutions and meted out the responsibilities.

Jim often had to privately field questions about this. How could the bombastic, arrogant, and quite frankly, not very smart Larry Fillmore risen in the cutthroat town of Washington DC to such a high position and stayed there all these years. In a word, it was Dolly. She had none of the necessary talents to be a Senator. Quiet, modest, and unassuming. But she had all the behind the scenes talents to make Larry Fillmore a star. Jim couldn't count the number of times the Senator had created unfixable disasters, only to have Dolly stroll in and solve the problem. She was an idiot savant. The kind that was a genius, but only in one specific area. In her case, that was saving her husband from ruin. She had the amazing ability to repair the catastrophes Senator Larry Fillmore managed to entangle himself in, and with only a few lines of input. That was why Jim continued, saying, "Yes, we have them in two dining rooms."

"Ah yes, those to live, and those to die." She had by now drifted to the window of the bridge that displayed XJ1, the rocket ship that held her husband. With her fingers lightly tapping the widow she said, "Did I say goodbye to the Senator? Think so. You have separated them, but what?"

"Well, we've got eleven people."

"Eleven?!" the Captain almost shouted, "I thought it was ten, and now the deal is off."

Ignoring the Captain's outburst, Jim said, "Eleven we want to get out of one of the dining rooms. Everyone inside knows what is going on. We can't get them out."

"Twelve," said Dolly calmly, "Now the number is twelve."

"Twelve? Huh lady? No let me…"

Dolly talked over the Captain, who became silent as she spoke. "Jim, I take it Barry is not aware of the food situation."

"Um, no… don't think so."

"Good, then he will be the perfect foil for us. He'll never give off the suspicion of something is up. We will use him to segregate our people from the rest, and as a bonus for doing so, he will be allowed to live. Plus, he is a big strong man. We'll need someone like that for this exercise maybe, and he's as big as they get."

"Look," said Captain Majewski, "We only got so much food, and these ten, eleven… hell, I don't care, thirty. There's no food allocated for them. Why there's no food for you."

"Jim? Can we handle the additions?"

"Hmmm… Think so."

"Good. Jim is always right about these things." As she said the words, Dolly didn't address them to the Captain, or anyone else for that matter. She might have been treated terribly by the Senator, but no one else dared such behavior. Dolly Fillmore always carried herself like a lady, and was treated as such in return. And rarely did she ever address anyone individually, even when speaking to them. There was an aura about her… that she was above the others. It had even been speculated that was the reason for the Senator's serial cheating. Either because he knew he was beneath her, or acted so badly trying to bring her down to his level. Whatever the reason, it had no effect on Dolly, who on Earth seemed as she now appeared in space, floating about on invisible winds that carried her, and her alone.

"Jim?"

"Yes?"

"The walkie-talkie."

Without saying a word, Jim obediently handed the walkie-talkie to Dolly, her eyes still focused on rocket ship XJ1. Without moving her hand she asked, "Is it on?"

Again Jim said nothing, choosing instead to bend over and fumble about the walkie-talkie in her hand until the volume clicked on.

Instantly Barry's voice could be heard, "What? Who the hell? Now listen…"

Pulling the walkie-talkie just before her lips Dolly said, "Is this Barry? Barry Wilson?"

"Yeah," was the response, already some of the bravado gone from his voice.

"This is Dolly Fillmore. I've spoken with the Senator. I have a job for you."

First there was silence as Dolly allowed the corners of her face to curl up in the slightest of confident smiles.

Barry said, "Yes ma'am."

"I want you to gather eleven people up. Do you understand?"

"Eh… yeah."

"If you don't want this assignment, then I'll have someone else. Do you want this?"

"Yes ma'am!" came the crisp voice of Barry, showing full respect and obedience.

"Good. I'm putting Jim on the line. He will provide the names. You are to gather them up and then take them to… just a moment."

Turning to the Captain she asked, where do you want them located?"

"Oh… yes, well I…"

Sneering slightly at the Captain, Dolly said, "Find out and then give that information to Jim. Jim you will pass it on to Barry. Understood?"

There was a unison of, "Yes ma'am," from both Jim and the Captain, very similar in tone to Barry's obedient response.

"Good… Jim." She extended out the walkie-talkie, indicating it was time for him to begin communicating with Barry. As Jim began to list the names of the twelve, Dolly returned her focus to the window and XJ1.

Gliding over Terri said sympathetically, "We have a line to XJ1… to the Senator, if you want."

Dolly glanced over at Terri before staring out the window once more. "No. He'll only try to get on board. Can't have that, can we? When he's focused on something, he doesn't listen, just yells."

"Yes but…"

Again Dolly glanced over at Terri, this time with some distain, before staring at XJ1. They were different, Dolly and Terri, and this was why Terri was an office worker married to an engineer, and Dolly had a Senator for a husband. "You must understand. We are it. There are no others."

"Ma'am?"

"Those other planets? Ships of fools. We are humanity, on this craft. Only two planets had any real hope for human survival, we are headed for one. No, my husband…" She stopped to consider what that word meant to her. "My husband had a wonderful life. Full and exciting. But he only wants what he wants. That was always his way. We best not have any more communication. They'll be desperate, like a wounded dog in a corner. Willing to do… to try anything. I loved him." She looked sincerely over at Terri, "I really did. But now, we are on opposite poles. I know it… and by now I think he knows as well. He can't be allowed on board, and that means we are not to communicate.

Terri looked out the window at XJ1, and couldn't help but ask, "Don't you have other family on board?"

Having returned to staring out the window, Dolly said, "The hatch… it's mangled… see?" She pointed at XJ1.

Terri squinted and could see the shiny white of the remainder of the hull of the docking room with metallic scratches on XJ1's bright red exterior. "How can you be so cruel?"

Dolly glanced sideways over at Terri. Smart girl… but never looked beyond her own nose. "I have a son… Lanny. My baby boy. He's on New Earth. Do I leave him there to die over some foolish plan to save those who are already dead? It's not like we can wait for a solution. Food is scarce and will be less soon enough. Even a day's delay might mean death, especially with the added bodies… thirteen including me." Then she added ominously, "And the longer we wait. The Senator doesn't take to losing easily."

Terri took another look at XJ1. What could that mean? Up until now, she had been hoping for a solution to the food shortage. Now she had a sudden urge to depart for New Earth, leaving XJ1 and the erratic and volcanic Senator behind.

Dining Room Breakout!

How difficult could it be? Get the twelve cordoned off, open the door, let them out, and lock the door again. Sounds simple. Unfortunately, the situation in dining room A was deteriorating similar to Earth below. As Barry began to segregate the twelve, there were first murmurs, then a few open complaints. Who were they? When Olga was placed in the group of the twelve, the words became more heated. She was Jim LaBlanc's wife. Already people had been killed, the thin chef had said as much. And when the thin chef made the cut, conspiracy theories abounded. Especially since the thin chef was chief in voicing complaints until selected.

But Barry was able to – through force, determination, and muscle – corral the other eleven and head for the door labeled "XX." Cramming down the button on the walkie-talkie Barry shouted, "Got them!"

"What's that screaming?"

"We got issues."

"Issues? What issues?" But Jim didn't have to ask. He could hear the screams of the others coming through the walkie-talkie.

His attention was diverted by Dolly, who said in a loud voice, "We've got a problem." Not exactly a loud voice, because Dolly never used such a tone. But slightly louder than normal, which was unheard of. Looking out the window she had perched beside, a finger was pointing out of the space station. As Jim and Captain Majewski slid over, Dolly said mildly, "They're going to ram us."

"What?" asked Captain Majewski, "That's suicide. Kill themselves."

"And us," added Dolly, "That's my Larry. If he can't, then no one can."

Shoving away from the window, Captain Majewski didn't bother to see if Dolly was right. XJ1 was short of fuel, but manned by a top notch Captain. He certainly had the talent to smash the rocket into the space station. The only way to avoid them was to maneuver away. In the distance he heard Jim say, "Yup. That's the plan. He's turning toward us."

On the walkie-talkie Barry barked, "Get the door open! It's getting nuts down here!"

Jim shouted at Gordon, "Come on!" As they passed the Captain, Jim said, "When we let you know. Unlock door "XX" got it? I'll get on the walkie talkie Barry has and give the word to lock the doors. I'm guessing shouldn't take more than twenty seconds. If you don't hear me by then. Lock the door. We can still close it, and once closed it will be locked."

Staring intently at the screen and franticly typing, the Captain mumbled, "Got it."

Shoving through the door to the dining rooms, Jim tossed the walkie-talkie to Terri asking, "How bout you?"

"Yeah. Wait for your signal… then when we hear your voice."

I'll pound on the wall, that's the signal to unlock. Gordon grab that." Jim pointed at a strip of flexible plastic about three feet long and as wide as a hand – some molding that had snapped off. And as they moved down the passageway Jim said, "I'll position you. When I'm in front of the door, you slap that against the wall. Then help me. It's going to be a jail break."

With a jerk, the entire ship shuddered as the jets were fired to put a spin on the space station once more. This time the jets remained on, and slowly the space station's rotation began to accelerate, moving a bit wobbly, due to rocket ship XJ2 being jammed against XJ4.

Reaching the corner of the hallway to dining room A, Jim slapped Gordon on the shoulder and said, "Here is good. Remember, when the door opens, come help."

Things may have been getting hectic on the space station, the situation on XJ1 was much calmer. Captain Boz was using the last of his fuel to carefully align the nose of his craft toward the SS 222. The Senator was still talking, but not as much now. Not since Captain Boz had smashed a fist in the Senator's face to express his displeasure with the Senator's constant complaints. Captain Boz had been in real combat, and if he was going to die, it wasn't going to be while listening to the constant whining of a snotty Senator.

In Captain Boz's opinion, it had come to this... and that was fine. He would charge SS 222, ramming it so that they might board, or failing that, everyone would die. He'd been there before. Sometimes you had to go all in. It might work, or it might not. So far, after all the craziness in his life, he was still breathing. Giving up and meekly watching the space station depart? That wasn't in him. As he saw the space station begin to spin, he mumbled, "That ain't gonna stop me buddy. We just need a little more adjustment, then it's time to dance."

Sitting next to Captain Boz, the Senator shifted in his seat uncomfortably and swallowed hard. He wanted on that ship, and if not. The hell with them. Let Captain Boz finish them all off.

Standing beside door "XX," Jim turned to Gordon shouting, "Now!"

As Gordon began to slap the plastic against the wall, Jim placed his hands on the door handle. Standing by the doorway to the bridge Terri heard the distant echoes. "That's it. That's our signal. Open the door."

"Ok, hang on," said Captain Majewski, "I just gotta..." He had already brought dining room A on the screen and quickly selected "file-options- doors-XX-open."

As he felt the "Cha-chunk!" of the door release, Jim yanked the door open and Terri counted slowly out loud, "One-two-three-four-five." Jim was grabbing people and yanking them into the hallway.

"Six-seven-eight-nine-ten."

Gordon had reached the door and stared to help pulling out the twelve. In the distance Jim could see the tuft of Olga's blond hair. "Olga! Come here!"

"Eleven-twelve-thirteen-fourteen-fifteen."

Everyone but Barry and Olga were out of the dining room, Olga still a ways away. First one person slipped past Jim, then another. Finally Barry was out.

"Sixteen-seventeen-eighteen-nineteen-twenty."

More people were rushing out, ten more… twenty, and still Olga was out of reach as the door lock clicked again, indicating that when the door closed, it would be secured. "Barry!" snarled Jim, "Barry!"

"Yeah?"

"Grab her! Grab the blond!"

Still more people squeezed past while Gordon tried to keep them in. Barry using his height, reached over and grabbed Olga by the hair on top of her head. As he pulled, he twisted her neck back to the point Jim was sure it was going to snap. To save Olga as much as anything else, Jim let more people through the door to make a path. As Barry managed to get two hands on her and pull her through the doorway Jim could see why it had been so difficult. She had her hands and legs wrapped around some unknown woman.

"Shut the door! Shut the Door!" shouted Jim. It took Jim, Barry, and Gordon, along with several of the other men outside to close the door, but finally it was sealed closed.

Angry, Jim stared at Olga and said, "What happened? You were supposed to be at the door."

Smiling in triumph Olga replied, "Yes, I was tryink to geet as many people oot as possible! Howt I do?"

Glaring at the mass of humanity surrounding him that would have to be fed, Jim's thought was to say, "You've killed us all." But then such a response wasn't possible, was it? Even if he had said so, Olga wouldn't understand. She was a true free spirit in all ways.

All he could manage was a lowly growled, "This is a problem."

Instantly upset by his words, Olga said, "My got Jim. You always the complainter. You figure it out. Always doot."

In his mind, Jim had no solutions to the death by starvation scenario formulating in his mind. Instead he could only imagine the expression of Captain Majewski upon learning they had an extra thirty to forty passengers more than expected. Staring around at the mass of humanity surrounding him… was it more?

On XJ1, Captain Boz had the rocket ship lined up for the final blast as the Senator groused, "I can't believe they'd do this to me. After all I'd done for them. They'd be dead and on Earth right now if not for me."

"Shut Up!" snapped Captain Boz. Being polite had got them nowhere. Now he was in control. He figured if he hit the food bins, they might be strong enough to hold the ship together and they could board. It was madness, but so was starving in outer space.

"You disagree?"

"Well I… I think." In his heart the Senator agreed, and completely. But it bothered him that his last act in life was not barking out orders, but rather sitting by while someone else – a lowly captain at that – made the decision that would likely end his existence.

"Exactly. Time to live… or time to die," said Captain Boz, a slightly maniacal grin on his face and excitement in his voice. He'd been to battle many times, and there was always – no matter the circumstances – some kind of charge to it. No doubt about it. He liked combat, action, and battle. With a mighty war whoop he slammed a fist on the remaining thruster with fuel. The passengers, hearing his scream, cheered back.

As the rocket lurched forward, Captain Majewski said, "We only got so much maneuverability. I can't outrun him. I'm too big… he's too quick."

"So then we're done for?" asked Terri.

"Pretty much, but we can try."

As the rocket began to accelerate toward the space station, Captain Majewski made his move, turning the energy indicators on all engines – nuclear and otherwise – to high. This was far too much and too early. It was one of the first things he learned in training regarding the nuclear engines on board SS 222. Until the core was sufficiently heated, no such risk should be attempted. But if they were rammed all was lost. As the space station began to push forward, Captain Majewski could see XJ1 adjusting it's path, a single flame of energy shooting from its side.

And then it happened. As Jim and Gordon returned to the bridge, at first the thrusting rocket on XJ1 flickered, and then went out. Came back on, and extinguished completely.

Seeing the rocket lose the last of it's engines, Captain Majewski encouraged, "Come on. Come on now." As XJ1 drifted toward SS 222, the space station began to rumble and shake as it accelerated. "That's it," said Captain Majewski, "We can make it."

Had XJ1 chosen the front of the ship as the point of impact, the nose of XJ1 would have pierced SS 222 somewhere in the midsection, most likely destroying SS 222. But having targeted the middle, first XJ1 drifted toward the tail… then deep space… as its path of trajectory glided past the rear of SS 222 by a good thirty feet. The space station would survive.

The Grim Reaper Is Summoned

"What do we do now?" asked Terri.

Gordon grabbed Terri by an arm and said softly, "Come on. Let's go."

Observing their departure, Dolly said, "I'll go along. The new passengers might need some calming."

The bridge was now empty, except for Jim and Captain Majewski. The two men stared at each other.

"Well," said the Captain.

Shaking his head no, Jim said, "Heavy is the head that wears the crown, *Captain*."

"What's that supposed to mean?"

"I'm just a bureaucrat. The grease that keeps the machine running."

"I don't get it."

"We need a leader. That was slated to be Senator Fillmore. That can't happen any more."

"So?"

"So Captain, "We need a leader. You said you want the job. If that's the case. I'll make sure to keep you safe, follow your orders, and hold on to your title and authority for you. But in exchange... leaders get the best of everything, but that's because they also have to do the worst."

Jim tapped on the computer keyboard. "You know what to do. What *you* have to do Captain. Sometimes decisions must be made where others must die... so that we can live."

Captain Majewski had no problems with such a role. That is until the moment arrived. The dining room was on screen. He simply had to execute the emergency protocol, removing the air from the room... leaving everyone inside dead. It had to be done. No other way. Looking at Jim, Captain Majewski asked, "You want to leave while I do it?"

Jim nodded no, saying, "I'll be honest, I can't do it. That's not me. But no man should have to take such a ride by himself. I'll be right here next to you... Captain."

"Huh?"

Pointing out of the cockpit, he said, "No. Look, out there."

Senator Fillmore didn't see anything. But Captain Boz, after decades of looking for small dots of color in a vast emptiness, first a fighter pilot, and now pilot of a rocket ship, was sure. He saw something. Grabbing his binoculars, he peered at a bright light beyond SS 222. It looked like a star, but didn't. It twinkled... but not like any star he'd seen. Focusing on the bright white dot, he adjusted his binoculars, and then again. Finally he pulled them away and asked, "SS 345, what's that?"

Seeming befuddled, Senator Fillmore said, "Just a maintenance craft."

"Looks kinda big to me."

"Yes, actually it was one of the first space centers, decided to be too small. Only holds a hundred or two. Not designed for deep space. Doesn't have the nuclear engines. Don't think so anyway."

After fiddling with his radio controls Captain Boz said, "SS 345, this is XJ1, over. Anyone on board?"

Crackling in the background came, "Yes XJ1, copy."

"What the hell you doing out here? Thought everyone was gone. We need emergency assistance, over."

"Don't look to us. We just found out. We got no food on board. Might have to return to Earth."

Captain Boz grinned. "Don't worry about that. I'm short of fuel. Can you assist?"

After a pause the response came, rather disinterested and distracted, "Sure. Ah... should be able to."

"Excellent. S'pose I can board?"

"Um, I guess, why?"

"Need to take a look at the hull, think I got a problem of some sort with the hatch."

"Yeah – sure."

"Thank you, over."

"Well," said Captian Boz happily, "Well, we got a ship. But no food."

Grinning back, Senator Fillmore said, "Yes we do. They're invited to dinner... just don't know it yet." Senator Fillmore laughed evilly at his cheap joke. He wasn't dead... not yet. Someone else would get that honor.